David S. Jordan, Joshua H. Stallard

The True Basis of Economics

The law of independent and collective human life; being a correspondence

between David Starr Jordan

David S. Jordan, Joshua H. Stallard

The True Basis of Economics
The law of independent and collective human life; being a correspondence between David Starr Jordan

ISBN/EAN: 9783337368548

Printed in Europe, USA, Canada, Australia, Japan

Cover: Foto ©Andreas Hilbeck / pixelio.de

More available books at **www.hansebooks.com**

THE TRUE BASIS

OF

ECONOMICS

OR

THE LAW OF INDEPENDENT AND
COLLECTIVE HUMAN LIFE

———

BEING A CORRESPONDENCE

BETWEEN

DAVID STARR JORDAN
President of the Leland Stanford Jr. University

AND

DR. J. H. STALLARD
Of Menlo Park, California

ON THE MERITS OF

THE DOCTRINE OF HENRY GEORGE

———

NEW YORK
DOUBLEDAY & McCLURE CO.

PREFACE.

This correspondence ensued on my request to Dr. David Starr Jordan, the President of Stanford University, that he would give me his opinion and comments on Henry George's letter to the Pope on the condition of labor.

It may be remembered that when the Rev. Dr. McGlynn, of New York, became a convert to the Single Tax, he was silenced by order of the Pope, and eventually excommunicated for contempt of his authority. The Pope then addressed an encyclical letter to his clergy, setting forth the principles involved in the labor problem as he saw them. To this Henry George replied in an open letter which was placed in the hands of the Pope himself. His Holiness apparently perceived that injustice had been done, and he ordered the reopening of Dr. McGlynn's case, with the result that he was restored to his duties in New York, the order of silence was withdrawn, and he was fully restored to the bosom of the Church.

Dr. Jordan promptly complied with my request, and in sending him my arguments in opposition to his views, I requested his permission to publish the correspondence, with such further comments as he might choose to make.

Dr. Jordan's answer is characteristic of the wise and open-minded man he is: "I have made many notes. Publish what seems to you not trifling or irrelevant and sign them (J), and add as many more as you please and sign them (S). The whole will be instructive and set folks thinking. That is all we college men are for."

That, too, is all that Single Taxers are for, and it is for the public to determine what is right.

For convenience the notes have been put in an appendix.

J. H. STALLARD, M. B.,

LONDON, ETC., ETC.

The Bungalow, Menlo Park,
San Mateo Co., Cal., May, 1899.

Dr. DAVID STARR JORDAN,

President Leland Stanford, Jr., University.

———

Dr. J. H. Stallard:—

There are many brilliant and many true things in Mr. George's book, and on the basis of His Holiness' assumption Mr. George gives him a very complete as well as a very courteous answer.

But as a whole, neither this nor any other of George's writings appeals to me. His whole basis seems faulty. He assumes that certain forms of property relation have a divine or sacred right. This assumption entering into his premises, reappears in his conclusions, which are thus regarded as proved, according to his logic. I deny every word of such premises, because I regard them as based on mere figures of speech. There is no such thing as a "right," except as we find experimentally that a certain line of action makes for more and better life among men. As regards the "law of equal access to land" among men, such a law is a mere figment, a mere metaphor. The trees have not equal access. While the present way of paying running expenses of government is very crude and faulty, and while a single tax would have several advantages, it has also its drawbacks, and a land tax is no more God-given than a beer tax.

Mr. George was a devoted man, had full faith in the sacredness of his mission, and he uses divine metaphors just as preachers do. The methods of science seem wholly unknown to him, and he falls back on his imaginary ethics whenever any one asks him how he would go to work to make land public property—whether, for example, by buying it or by seizing it, or by alone taxing ownership out of existence, and as to how any of these methods could be made to work. Property is not a divine right. It is a creation of social agreement, and the relation best for society is "right" if we can find it out.

If, as Dr. Warner says, "putting air in private hands would yield a better supply on juster terms, there is no divine reason why we should not turn the atmosphere over to an air company."

Take George's work, squeeze out every metaphor, cut out all this stuff from the French dreamers of the last century about the rights of man to one thing or another, and put it all into straight English. You would have considerable practical sense about various men and things drawn from his own extensive observations; but the argument from divine right and the purposes of nature has not a straw's weight, namely: that men have a natural right to access to land; therefore, all taxes must by divine authority be laid on land rentals.

I am not objecting to the idea of the public use of land rentals, but to the divine or metaphysical argument in its favor. The only true argument must be this: It has been tried, it works, and its results on individual and social development are better than those obtained through other forms of land tenure and of taxation. I do not believe this, either, but I am reasonably open to conviction. Argument from purpose, intention or divine fitness is a mere quibble of words.

DAVID STARR JORDAN.

Dr. J. H. STALLARD,

The Bungalow, Menlo Park, Cal.

DEAR DR. JORDAN:—

I have to thank you for your prompt reply to my request for your opinion of Henry George's address to the Pope on the condition of labor.

You are a prince among educators, the head of the most liberal university in the world—an institution which I trust under your leadership shall become the home of all freedom, and whose professors and students shall determine the lines of action which shall hereafter make for more and better life among men, for which there is more than ample room. I therefore regard the expression of your views on this, as on all intellectual, social, and political questions on which you choose to speak, as the truest representation of modern thought of the highest type, and I shall endeavor to discuss the subject in hand in all seriousness and with due respect.

You say, "That the whole basis of Mr. George's argument is faulty; that he assumes that certain forms of property relation have a divine or sacred right, and that his premises are based upon mere figures of speech. Take George's work, squeeze out every metaphor, cut out all the 'stuff' of the French dreamers of the last century about the rights of man to one thing or another, and put it all into straight English, the argument would not have a straw's weight. In his logic he takes out nothing at the end not assumed at the beginning."

In the following observations I propose to squeeze out every metaphor, every suggestion of divine authority and the purposes of nature, all the "stuff" of the French dreamers of the last century, to confine myself to the most strictly scientific methods, and, in straight English, to base my argument on facts established by human observation and experience about which there is absolutely no room for doubt.

Before doing so I desire to thank you for your good and terse definition of what is "right," and I agree "that there is no such thing as 'right' except as we find experimentally that a certain line of action makes for more and better life among men." I promise faithfully to apply this definition to every conclusion I may draw.

THE LAW OF INDEPENDENT HUMAN LIFE.

In the first place, man is an animal endowed with "intelligence" and "strength,"[1] which, in active combination is technically called "labor." Labor exerted upon earth, air, water and sunshine, technically called "land," yields the product "food," on which "all men" live. The application of labor to land is technically called "industry"[2] in the following argument.

These simple indisputable facts form the whole foundation of Mr. George's argument. There is in these premises no metaphor, no mere figures of speech, no "if," no assumption of divine right or purposes of nature, but a simple, truthful and unanswerable statement of man's dependence on the voluntary exercise of his own powers upon "land," on the result of which he lives and maintains existence. Here then we have a statement of bare, undoubted facts, involving a simple line of action, which not only makes for more and better life among men but is the only possible foundation for the continuance of human life.

In the next place, that which is true of the whole is true of the several parts upon which this line of action operates. Man finds experimentally that he must have under his own individual control intelligence, strength and land, none of which can be taken from him without the destruction of his life. There is no experimental evidence that human life can be continuously maintained in any other way.[3] Man cannot live on intelligence, nor on strength, and "food" will not drop into his open mouth.[4] This line of action being open, man's independent life depends solely on his own voluntary exertion. If a man will not work, neither shall he eat, and the penalty of idleness is death. Happily "industry" is as natural as "sleep" to healthy, well-fed men, and the gate of independence is thus made open.

You have lately taught us wisely that the maintenance and development of manhood is the most important matter which any nation in the world has now on hand, and that each man must help to solve his own problems. The independent maintenance of his own life is for each man the first and most important problem. The manhood of a nation depends on the manhood of its units. The conditions of the problem are embodied in the line of action evolved from the facts detailed. A man has only to be free to think, free to act, and free to take maintenance by his own labor from the land, and the problem for the individual is solved. His life, therefore, depends on the active combination of intellectual, personal, and industrial freedom. There is no other way. No man is free who under any condition whatever is compelled to beg of another either food or work.[5] Absolute individual freedom depends on "self employment," only made possible by "access to land," which is, therefore, no "*mere figment*," but an essential condition in the maintenance of independent human life.[6] Lastly, justice between man and man declares the equal right of every man to the products of his own labor. It constitutes his wealth and is the foundation upon which his freedom rests. It is his to consume, to hoard or dispose of at his will, and no one has either legal or moral right to take it from him without his consent and adequate compensation.

Your argument that the trees have not "equal access" to land seems to me without force.[7] The life of trees is not dependent on the same conditions as the life of man. Trees are not endowed either with intellect or active strength.[8] They have no power of choice or locomotion, both of which are absolute conditions of individual human life. Besides "*equal*" access is neither possible nor necessary either to trees or man. Equal opportunity is all that is required. Once armed with the independent opportunity of maintaining life by the employment of his own "labor" upon "land" a man however destitute is really "free."[9] He is no longer at the mercy of employers.[10] He is no longer subject to the law of Lasalle. Henceforth he is provided with an alternative which enables him to refuse "*bare subsistence wages*," and he possesses an independent remedy against starvation, misery and death. He is provided with a line of action which experimentally makes for more and better life among men.[11]

In the next place, this "line of action" is inexorable, unalterable, and universal in its application. There is no other "line of action" which secures the independent existence of human beings. It rises, therefore, to the conditions of "a general law." This law of independent life controls the maintenance of human life and movements just as the law of gravitation controls the life and movements of the planetary bodies. Starvation, misery and death result from the violation of the one, as surely as planetary destruction would from the violation of the other.[12]

Now, general laws are laws of necessity, morality and justice. In action they are just, equal, unchangeable and permanent. There is, therefore, no room for that fickle, unstable, undefined and mythical force called "Social Agreement," which is wholly unable to determine what is "right," and it is no wonder that "rights" so artificially created are difficult, nay, impossible, to find out. Social agreement cannot be a substitute for a general law, for no statesman is wise enought, no government strong enough, to improve on such a law. Social agreement can only meddle with intellectual, personal and industrial freedom, to spoil their just and equal action. Social agreement is impotent to provide either food or employment for all mankind.[13] History provides us with many examples of its baneful interference. In the reign of Henry VII, when in England "every rood maintained its man," the English yeoman occupied his rood in comfort and happiness on definite and easy terms.[14] But when Henry VIII made land a commodity to be bought, sold, and controlled by individuals (called Steplords by Latimer), the masses of the people were evicted from their homesteads by the exaction of rent they could not pay. In a few years the whole island swarmed with the destitute, who became vagabonds and thieves in order to sustain existence. The nation was threatened with anarchy, and in the reign of Elizabeth social agreement, as represented by the English Poor Law, endeavored to remedy the evil, by giving to the destitute a legal right to food, clothing and shelter, making this a first charge upon the land. The result was pauperism; the greatest curse ever inflicted upon a thrifty and industrious people.[15]

After 300 years the sermons of Latimer are re-echoed by Mr. Henry George, and happily their doctrines will never again be stifled at the stake.

In Spain, social agreement attempted to control

the intellects of men, and the result was the miseries, tortures and murders of the Inquisition.

In America and elsewhere social agreement sought to control personal freedom, and the result was "slavery."

And to-day social agreement continues the practice of that tyrant, Henry. Still treats land as a commodity of sale and purchase. Still gives the landlord power to exact a steadily increasing rent. Still gives him power to evict those who refuse or are unable to pay him toll. Still enables the landlord to live in ease and luxury on the labor of other people, and make serfs and paupers of the industrial class.

The conclusion is unanswerable, social agreement cannot successfully control the conditions of independent human life, the only fixed law which makes experimentally for more and better life among men.[16]

THE LAW OF COLLECTIVE HUMAN LIFE.

Now, the law of independent human life is also the law of human life in general. That which is true of "all men" in the individual sense must also be true of "all men" in the collective sense. All men collectively must have intellectual, personal, and industrial freedom, which are, therefore, the essential elements of both individual and collective life. The law of individual life is simply fortified and extended by collective action. Thus whilst individual industrial freedom secures for "all men" individually little more than a *"bare subsistence,"* collective industrial freedom is able to satisfy the millions of intellectual and physical desires of "all men" living in civilized communities; and if this result is not reached, the failure cannot be charged upon the law but on its violation and neglect. As access to land is an essential element of individual life and freedom, so it must be an essential element of collective life and freedom, for without land no community can live or find material on which to operate.[17] It is this inseparable relation of land to labor which gives the land such paramount importance, for unless "land" be equally free to all mankind, industrial freedom becomes impossible both to individuals and to mankind in general.

Again, as the law of independent life secures to every individual the products of his own industry, to consume, to hoard, or dispose of at his will, so the law of collective life demands co-partnership in the products of collective industry, to be hoarded, consumed or disposed of by the collective will. The collective operators cannot appropriate and use the products of individual industry nor can individuals appropriate and use the products of collective industry. Either violates the general law of human life, which makes for more and better life among men. From this it follows that wherever there is co-operation in production, there must also in justice be co-partnership in result, and both become equally essential elements of the general law of human life. The nation, state, city or community which takes the products of individual labor without his consent and adequate compensation destroys individual freedom, and acts like a thief who robs him of the same, and as this is done by modern governments, they fail to make for more and better life among men.

On the other hand, every individual who appropriates the products of collective labor, and thus denies co-partnership in the collective result, is equally guilty of robbing the collective units. As this also is sanctioned and upheld by modern governments they fail on both accounts to make for more and better life among men.

Now, it is not difficult to discover the source of collective products, nor where they go. They spring from the fact that in collective industry no individual can work for himself *exclusively*, because the combined industry of two or more men is necessarily stronger and more efficient than that of the same two or more men acting separately each in his own behalf. Therefore, after awarding to each individual that portion of the collective product which represents his individual exertion (technically called his wages) there is invariably a surplus produced by the co-operators in their corporate capacity, in which, nevertheless, the individuals have a co-partnership interest.[18] In the millions of complicated conditions of collective life and labor it is impossible to segregate the share of each producer in the collective result, but it is universally admitted that the larger part is faithfully conserved and concentrated in land value, and that it constitutes that increment of value which attaches to land in consequence of the increase of population, and is technically called "rent."[19] Without collective industry land has no value and there is no "rent"—which "coeteris paribus" increases directly in proportion to the population. It is the collective industry of the population which alone produces it. It is the population who are co-partners and who are authorized by the general law of human life to hoard, consume or dispose of as they please, and as it cannot be equitably divided amongst the individual producers, it can only be applicable to the provision of their common wants, of which the current expenses of government is a fair example. Hence it is the only source of taxation provided by the general law of human life. It is the "Single Tax."

The result of this analysis of Mr. Henry George's premises justifies the conclusion that it is only by absolute obedience to the general law of independent and collective human life that we can hope to realize the inalienable right of all men equally to life, liberty and the pursuit of happiness (Jefferson), the satisfaction of human, intellectual and physical desires (H. George), or the making for more and better life among men (Jordan).

LAND APPROPRIATION.

Having thus established the general law of independent and collective human life which "all men" must obey in order to live and prosper, it is permitted by the accepted canon of scientific procedure to substitute the "deductive" for the "inductive" method, and to employ the general law as to the test of existing conditions and as a means of pointing out other lines of action which make for more and better life among men.

And first with regard to "land." In order to state these conditions clearly I will relate a recent history of land appropriation.

Within a few weeks of fifty years ago, a few hundred citizens of the United States landed on the western shore of San Francisco Bay. They found a nest of sterile sand-hills of no more value than the summits of the Sierra Nevada Mountains.

They were free to take, and did take, all the surface they required for use. But not content with
this, and under the paramount power and authority of the Government of the United States,
the most perfect organization of social agreement
in the world, they proceeded to appropriate to
themselves and their heirs and assigns forever the
exclusive ownership of "all the earth in sight."

Had these citizens raised the peninsula from the
depths of the Pacific Ocean by their own associated labor, the land would have been their own,
and this appropriation would have been fully jus-
tified; but as they found the sand-hills ready to
their hands, it seems difficult to understand how
any authority whatever or any deed or paper could
confer upon any set of individuals the exclusive
ownership of one of the essential conditions of
human life, and of a portion of the earth specially
adapted to the conditions of collective life.

But in accordance with the law, they divided up
the land into blocks, and the public official who
conducted the appropriation still lives in San
Francisco, and testifies that many hundreds of
these blocks were given away to individuals without the payment of a cent, without even any guarantee to use them, and at the sole cost of pens, ink
and paper necessary for the completion of this
strictly *"legal,"* and according to jurists, states-

men and political economists, strictly *"righteous"* action.[20]

That the land was valueless does not in any way alter the nature of the case. These citizens were legally created "landlords," and given absolute control of what was already a necessity of associated life. They were endowed with the power of making serfs of "all men" who should hereafter desire to occupy *"their land."* In straight English they were simply "landgrabbers," legalized thieves of land which they did not make, and to the use of which they had no better title than any other set of men. They took advantage of the unrighteous law and practice of the United States to forestall the advent of an industrious population, already known to be on the way to San Francisco from every quarter of the globe; and to make all future immigrants pay toll for the privilege of occupying these easily acquired "blocks," or to pay purchase money for the transfer of the right to collect this toll. These robbers are still at large, and still enjoy the protection of the "law" ! ! They, their heirs and assigns, still continue to exact a steadily increasing toll for the privilege of occupation; still have the right to sell at a continually advancing price. Many of these landgrabbers withhold their blocks from use, because they are certain that with increasing population their value will increase, and will ensure more rent. Nor is this practice confined to city "blocks." Millions of acres in the State of California are held by "landgrabbers" on the same title, not so much for present use and profit as for the prospective certainty that an increase of population will give them higher rent or more purchase money for the privilege of taking it.

But the "cinch" of these "landgrabbers" was not exclusively confined to land considered as a place of residence. For he who controls the land controls the laborer who lives on it. From the moment of this appropriation, fifty years ago, until to-day, these landgrabbers have exacted toll from every laborer. Every coming ship brought more grist to the grabbing mill. Every man who did an hour's work, built a shanty, opened a store, or made a workshop; every importer who brought in food and clothing, increased the value of their unoccupied, sterile blocks. And now every improvement, whether made by individuals, corporations, or the city government, brings gain to the grabbers of the rent. If a street is well paved, well lighted, and well cleansed by the public servants, the rent of the houses will be higher than that of similar houses in a dirty, dark and ill paved street. A park created at the public cost raises the rental of the surrounding land. Car lines have recently been constructed on two streets of San Francisco, and the abutting land assessment has been raised fifty per cent., all of which is, or will be, made the source of increased rent. The necessities of commerce have raised the value of land on the water front; the requirements of retail business have done the same on Market street. Residential value is continually growing in the suburbs; and to-day a square foot of land in San Francisco is worth more than a hundred square miles upon the mountain tops. That which was valueless fifty years ago is now worth many hundred millions.[21] Here then is a huge fund, not created by these so-called owners, but by the co-operate activities and necessities of the entire community. A fund which under the general law of associated human life belongs to the co-partners who produced it, to be administered by social agreement for public purposes and in the interest of all the people.

A fund which has been diverted from it lawful owners to the pockets of men whose individual industry scarcely contributed a mite to the result. A fund which has enabled thousands to live in idleness and luxury at the expense of the poverty, misery and starvation of their fellow citizens.

Consider for a moment what this co-partnership fund would have done for its real owners. The current expenses of the municipal, state and federal governments would have been a mere bagatelle. The municipal government might have erected gas works, water works, electrical works, and street car lines. Light, electricity, water and public transportation might have been free to all, whereas, these works have been erected by capital furnished by the rent belonging to the citizens and for the use of which the citizens now must pay. Public buildings not dreamed of in the palmy days of Greece and Rome could have been erected at the public cost; also, free schools, universities, libraries, theatres, museums, art galleries, parks and observatories; and a score of public utilities by which the co-partner profits might have been indefinitely increased. And at our public festivals we could have emulated the citizens of Potosi, by paving our streets with silver and adorning our public processions with gold and precious stones. And all this without taking one cent of taxation from individual industry. It is impossible to conceive the effect of the Single Tax on the morals and intellectual progress of the people, but it may be safely stated that the fear of poverty being gone the need of policemen, judges, jails, and poorhouses would have been reduced to a minimum.[22]

Tested experimentally the existing relation between land and population is a grievous violation of the general law of human life. The vast fund created by co-operative industry, the administration of which belongs to the population as co-partners, has been diverted by social agreement to individuals who have no claim. It is the object of the "Single Tax" to restore this fund to the control of its original producers, and thus relieve industry of the millstone of rent hung about its neck by landlords. Thus giving individual and collective workers the full enjoyment of the wealth they respectively produce. The fulfillment of the general law of human life is the only line of action which makes for more and better life among men.

CONFUSION AS TO PROPERTY IN LAND.

And here I have to note your statement "that Mr. George falls back on his imaginary ethics whenever anyone asks him how he would make 'land' public property, whether by buying it or seizing it, or taxing ownership out of existence, or how any of these methods could be made to work." I am indeed grieved to notice so complete a misapprehension of Mr. George's doctrine. There is throughout Mr. George's writings no proposal whatever to make land public property by buying it or seizing it, and, consequently, no attempt at explanation as to how either method could be made to work. On the contrary, he states that a redivision of land is not possible, and if possible could not be permanent. That possession for use is necessary for the sower to reap his crop, or the builder to recoup the cost of the improvements he may make. He nowhere proposes to disturb the present occupiers of land; and insists that any such disturbance would amount to revolution.

You seem to confound property in use with property in so-called ownership; and to suppose that ownership is necessary for land improvement and development. But this is not even a general experience. Half London, including many hundreds of its finest palaces, half New York, and of many other cities have been constructed on land not owned by the builders.[23] The landlords of London and New York are not such fools as to alienate their perpetual right to constantly increasing rent. It remains only to governments like that of the United States to give away the national heritage for the price of pens, ink and paper, and enable landlords forever to collect a continually increasing toll on labor. It is quite true that Mr. George rests most of his arguments on the foundation of moral right, as when he states that a laborer is entitled morally to the products of his own industry. And there are thousands who believe that this is the stronger ground, but a close analysis distinctly proves that his ethics are not imaginary, and that his metaphors are supported by substantial facts, namely, those laid down at the beginning of this letter.

Instead of demanding an accounting such as would be ordered by the Courts in the case of individuals wrongfully[24] possessed of land, Mr. George proposes to let by-gones be by-gones, and the landlord having had his turn it is now more than time that the people, who have been so long defrauded of the product of their collective labor, and have suffered so deeply for the want of the "rent" which they have earned, should be restored to their collective heritage.

Mr. George's proposal is just, clear and practical. He desires that "all men" in their collective capacity should assume their undoubted right to the ownership of land, and that all men individually shall have equal opportunity to its use and occupation on the payment of rent representing its value to the entire community. This rent to be collected as a single tax, and used to provide for common necessities and the satisfaction of common desires. The result, no doubt, will be the ultimate destruction of the landlord—a consummation devoutly to be wished.

But Mr. George did not expect that the "rent" could be taken from the landlords all at once.

They are much too powerful, and the masses of producers much too ignorant and venal. But the time is coming, and it is not far distant, when the producers of wealth shall have learned their "rights" under the general law of human life, and with the aid of universal suffrage and the ballot will not fail to take them. It is the duty of universities to conduct the necessary change with wisdom and moderation.

THE PRESENT CONDITION OF LABOR.

Mr. George, in Progress and Poverty, described the present condition of the laborer in the lowest ranks of civilized society, whose life is spent in common labor, or in producing one thing or an infinitesimal part of one thing, out of the multiplicity of things that constitute the wealth of society. How he is a mere link in the enormous chain of producers and consumers; helpless to separate himself, and helpless to move except as they move. The worse his position in society the more he is dependent on society, the more utterly unable does he become to help himself.

The very power of exerting his labor for the satisfaction of his most reasonable wants passes from his own control, and may be taken away or restored by the action of others, or by general causes, over which he has no more influence than he has over the motions of the solar system. That under such circumstances he loses the essential quality of manhood. He becomes a slave, a machine, a commodity, a thing in some respects lower than the animal, for he looks to crime and drunkenness as the only hopeful sources of relief.

In the days of cannibalism, says Ingersoll, the strong devoured the weak, actually ate their flesh. In spite of all the laws that man has made, in spite of all the advances of science, the strong still live upon the weak,[25] the unfortunate, the foolish. True, they do not eat their flesh and drink their blood, but they live on their labor. The man who deforms himself by toil, who labors for his wife and children through all his barren wasted life, and goes to his grave without having tasted a single luxury, has been the food of others. The poor woman living in her lonely room, cheerless and fireless, sewing night and day to keep starvation from her child, is slowly being eaten alive by her fellow men.[26] When I take into consideration the agony of civilized life, the failures and anxieties, the tears and withered hopes, the bitter realities, the hunger,[27] crime, drunkenness, ignorance and humiliation, I am almost forced to say that cannibalism, after all, is the most merciful form in which man has lived upon his fellow men.

In this connection Markham's great poem recently written, after seeing Millet's famous picture of The Man With the Hoe, deserves quotation:

Bowed by the weight of centuries he leans
Upon his hoe and gazes on the ground,
The emptiness of ages in his face,
And on his back the burden of the world.
Who made him dead to rapture and despair,
A thing that grieves not and that never hopes,
Stolid and stunned, a brother to the ox?
Who loosened and let down this brutal jaw?
Whose was the hand that slanted back this brow?
Whose breath blew out the light within this brain?

Is this the thing the Lord God made and gave
To have dominion over all the land;
To trace the stars and search the heavens for
    power;
To feel the passion of Eternity?
Is this the Dream He dreamed who shaped the suns
And pillared the blue firmament with light?
Down all the stretch of Hell to its last gulf
There is no shape more terrible than this—
More tongued with censure of the world's blind
    greed—
More filled with signs and portents for the soul—
More fraught with menace to the universe.

What gulfs between him and the seraphim!
Slave of the wheel of labor, what to him
Are Plato and the swing of Pleiades?
What the long reaches of the peaks of song,
The rift of dawn, the reddening of the rose?
Through this dread shape the suffering ages look;
Time's tragedy is in that aching stoop;
Through this dead shape humanity betrayed,
Plundered, profaned and disinherited,
Cries protest to the Judges of the world,
A protest that is also prophecy.

O, masters, lords and rulers in all lands,
Is this the handiwork you give to God,
This monstrous thing distorted and soul-quenched?
How will you ever straighten up this shape;
Give back the upward looking and the light;
Rebuild it in the music and the dream;
Touch it again with immortality;
Make right the immemorial infamies
Perfidious wrongs, immediable woes?

O, masters, lords and rulers in all lands,
How will the future reckon with this man?
How answer this brute question in that hour
When whirlwinds of rebellion shake the world?
How will it be with kingdoms and with Kings—
With those who shaped him to the thing he is—
When this dumb error shall reply to God,
After the silence of the centuries?

———

This the truest and most forcible accusation ever launched by genius against the existing conditions of society. It is a fitting climax to Hood's "Song of the Shirt," Burns' "O'er Labored Wight" and Mrs. Browning's impassioned cry to "Hear the Children Weeping."

These only describe the pitiable facts, but the great merit of Markham's poem consists in his pointing out the cause, and its inestimable value lies in the fact that when the cause of any great evil becomes known and recognized by the masses of the people it is sure to be removed.

Oh, landlords, masters, and rulers of the soil, is this the handiwork you give to God? It is by you humanity has been betrayed, plundered, profaned and disinherited. It is you who have shaped him

31

to be the thing he is. How shall it be with you when this dumb terror shall reply to God after the silence of the centuries? The man with the hoe is not a remnant of prehistoric times. The knowledge of good and evil was man's first acquirement, a knowledge which the man with the hoe has lost. Barbarism never made a human being like him. No such creature is to be found among savage races. He is not a simple improvement on the monkey taught to use the hoe. His ancestors were men, not monkeys. He is the natural brother of the honored among men, La Place, Des Cartes, Pasteur and a thousand others.

He is not exclusively of French production. In many countries he is found in the garb of woman. He is found abundantly in Eastern Germany, where landlords are strong and powerful. Throughout England he is found in the very midst of civilization, and he is known in every village. His name is Hodge, and he is recognized by the ingenious deliberation of all his movements, for he has learned by dire experience to accurately adapt his expenditure of force to the measure of his bare subsistence diet. In the presence of his master he puts forth a little deceptive energy, but behind his back he rests upon his hoe and looks upon the ground. Moreover, he is here the last to escape from military service. He is the easy prey of the recruiting sergeant. He takes the Queen's shilling in prospect of a mild debauch. He struts like a peacock in his scarlet uniform. Set up and drilled he becomes the sturdy backbone of the great military machine. In the ranks he is the ignorant but faithful comrade of the intelligent but more weakly soldiers drawn from the factories and slums. Endowed with the hereditary courage of the bull dog he attacks the enemy in front, and does not know when he is whipped. He is too big a fool to run away, and after he is prepared as food for powder he dies upon the battlefield without a murmur. Hodge was not created by the removal of the strong but by the pressure of the crafty on the weak. He is the victim of generations of ill usage and unceasing labor. Heredity has stamped ignorance upon his mind and brutal degeneration on his body. He is the production of retrogressive evolution. This type is found in various forms, and more or less developed in every rent ridden country upon earth, wherever landlords are privileged by law to suck out the brains and life blood of the people, and make them slaves of rent. The masters of the soil have fed upon his labor without shame or mercy, and have left him nothing but the hoe and bare subsistence. He was created man, and has been made a brute by uncontrollable social forces. Worse housed than the ox—stalled like the ox—goaded like the ox, he toils from early dawn till late at night. Like the ox he feeds and sleeps only to be able to renew his labors. Stolid and stunned he becomes dead to rapture and despair, a thing that grieves not, and that never hopes. From all the stretch of hell to its last gulf, there is no shape more terrible, more tongued with censure of the world's blind greed, more fraught with menace to the peace of all nations and the universe.

These then are faithful descriptions of industrial bondage.[28] A bondage fastened down by the so-called law of wages tending to bare subsistence point. The law of wages described by Mill as "natural,"[29] the "iron law" which bears the indorsement of the very highest names amongst professors of political economy. A law taught in text books, schools, and universities throughout the world; and yet, for all this, a law which has falsehood and damnation written on its very face. For it cannot be denied that every known general law of nature makes for more and better life among men,[30] whilst this, the creation of social agreement, makes for starvation, misery and death. The facts afford the strongest condemnation of the so-called law. And who are the cannibals who slowly eat up the lives and labor of the laboring classes? Who takes the wealth they

individually and collectively produce? Are they
not governments, landlords, millionaires, trusts
and corporations?[21] Controlled by these selfish
cormorants, social agreement, by obstructing "access to land," has knocked the bottom out of industrial freedom, and is able to drive wages down,
down, down, until the "bare subsistence" point is
reached,and only stops there because death putsan
end to further robbery, and casts upon the cannibals the cost of burial. And notice the result.
In England one and a half per cent. of the adult
population own eighty per cent. of the wealth,
while eighty-seven and a half per cent. of the
adult working poor own only two per cent. In
America nine per cent. of the adult population
own seventy-one per cent. of the wealth, and sixty-
three per cent. of the adult working poor own no
more than nine per cent. The American cannibals
have made good time in a hundred years and bid
fair soon to overtake their English cousins.[32]

Now, the industrial bondage of civilized human
life is worse than that of chattel slavery. The
slave was, at least, well cared for. He had the
possibility of escape. There were lands in which
he would be free. But the industrial slaves of
modern life are made responsible for their own
existence on a "bare subsistence" scale. In spite
of education, in spite of individual skill and per-

sistent industry and thrift, not one in ten thousand can escape. Hundreds of thousands lose their health and lives in the hopeless struggle, and leave to their children the heritage of weakened constitutions.[33] In cities like London and New York whole streets are inhabited by adults with children's powers, children's ignorance, children's constitutions, earning children's wages, living on children's food, with children's ambitions, and yet without children's prospects of becoming men. The cannibals have eaten out the hearts of such communities, and left the husk to wither still on "bare subsistence" law. What a mockery to tell these people, taxed to death, that they can improve their condition by education, industry and thrift. There is no possible escape from such bondage. Go where they will the "bare subsistence" wage will follow them. The landlord will deny them the use of land without the payment of his rent. The capitalist, whilst giving the "bare subsistence" wages, robs them of their collective industry, and in proportion as population and civilization grow in new countries so does industrial bondage fasten on the people. But, as in the East, nineteen centuries ago, the morning star of love heralded the coming of the Great Prophet of universal brotherhood, that bond of co-partnership which is an essential element of the law of human life, so to-day has the western evening star of industrial freedom heralded the prophet of material prosperity and comfort as the outcome of obedience to the same great law.

The prophet of California has forged the hammer which shall remove the fetters of industrial bondage and given the world the key which shall open the door to industrial freedom. Ridiculed by professors of political economy, despised by modern Scribes and Pharisees, rejected by the Priests of Christian churches, and denounced by ignorant politicians, he spent a noble life, and suffered death in the cause of humanity.[34] But he brought glad tidings of great joy to suffering millions and the people heard him gladly. Already, after less than twenty years, the gospel of "Single Tax" has been preached in every civilized community, and his disciples number millions.[35]

In England seven millions of co-operative and co-partner workers, the pick of the industrial community, are followers of Henry George. For years past the great convention of English laborers, the most numerous, most intellectual and most powerful labor organization in the world, has passed resolutions in favor of the taxation of land value (the Single Tax). And already the leading liberal statesmen are following suit. John Morley has declared that the taxation of land value will be an issue at the next election. He is supported by Lord Roseberry, Sir Wm. Vernon Harcourt, Earl Carrington, Professor James Bryce and the Hon. Henry Asquith. Among the members of the English House of Commons are Billson of Halifax, Pirie of Aberdeen, Sinclair of Forfar, Cameron of Glasgow, McGhee of South Meath, and Michael Davitt of Ireland, all of whom have been elected on the platform of the Single Tax. In Canada the workmen's conventions have annually adopted "Single Tax," and Sir Wilfred Laurier, the Premier, says that all future legislation must be carried forward on the line of the "Single Tax."

And now curiously Germany, the most conservative power in Europe, has established the Single Tax as the only source of revenue in the most backward country in the world. In the new colony of Kiautchou, in China, the Minister of Marine made the following statement, "no colony has ever enjoyed such absolute freedom of production and trade as we have secured to Kiautchou. Not one single duty or tax will be imposed, except the taxes on land values. This measure has been dictated solely by politic-economical considerations." That the measure is popular is proved by the petiton presented to the British Government by the merchants, who are also land owners of Hong Kong, who, led by Mr. Mathieson, proposed the abolition of all taxes and the substitution for the same of taxes on land values.

Even in America men like Mr. Thomas G. Sherman of New York, and the Hon. Tom L. Johnson vie with that old veteran of freedom—Wm. Lloyd Garrison—in advocating the Single Tax, whilst in New Zealand and New South Wales the principle is acknowledged and acted upon by both governments. This is a pretty good showing for a theory founded on "mere figures of speech" and an argument not worth "a straw's weight."[37]

THE LAND TAX AND BEER TAX.

We are now prepared to discuss the question of paying the running expenses of government of which you say, "While the present way of paying the running expenses of government is very crude and faulty, and while the 'Single Tax' would have several advantages, it has also its drawbacks, and a land tax is no more God-given than a beer tax." But we have agreed that it is not a question whether God favors a land tax or a beer tax, although many would affirm that a beer tax would probably have the preference. There is, at least, one substantial difference between them. Land is not a product of human industry, whilst beer is, and this fact alone may determine which of the two is the better subject of taxation. The real question is which will most equitably distribute the burden of taxation among all the tax payers, which will interfere least with industrial freedom and most favor the same in the larger field of collective industry? Which, in fact, is in most complete accord with the general law[38] of human life, the only law which makes for more and better life among men?[39]

As "all men" derive their independent and collective lives, comforts, necessities and luxuries from land it follows that a tax on land value reaches every living being in proportion to the use he makes of it.

The individual living and acting by himself and for himself alone, contributes nothing to land value, and is not called upon to pay running expenses of a collective government in which he has no place, and of which he has no need.[40] But as soon as a government is needed by a growing population rent is created, and the law of co-partnership, a most just and equitable law, steps in to determine that the collective product shall be set apart for collective use, of which current expenses of government are a part, and just as the needs of the population increase with increased population the fund expands[41] to meet their increased common wants. This seems to me a most wise and equitable arrangement, whereby the back is fitted to the burden, and the industry of individuals is set free to secure for themselves the full products of their individual exertion, and to pursue happiness by the gratification of their intellectual and physical desires. Surely this is an arrangement which makes for more and better life among men.[42]

On the other hand, beer is a product of individual and collective industry. It requires the co-operation of farmers, malsters, brewers, coopers, wagoners and a thousand other people to produce and distribute a single glass. Rent is the surplus of their collective industry from which the single tax is paid. Thus beer pays its proportion of taxation, leaving individual exertion free. But to pay a tax on beer directly is a violation of the law of individual freedom which secures for every laborer the absolute possession and disposal of the product of his own exertion;[43] that is, without licenses, taxation or other interference by social agreement with the gratification of individual desires.

Nor is there any moral reason for a beer tax. Beer has been adopted by all civilized nations as a drink well suited to satisfy thirst and their civilized desires. It has been selected under the law of evolution, just as wheat, rice, meat and other articles of diet. It is not in use by the stagnant and effete nations of the earth—Turks, Arabs, Hindoos and Chinese. For centuries it has formed the principal drink of the Anglo-Saxon race. Less than a hundred years ago, when tea and coffee were but little known, and less used, our ancestors drank beer for breakfast, beer for dinner, beer at supper, and beer at all their festivals. It was in universal use by all who could afford to brew or buy it. And with this habit the race has colonized the earth and become the leaders of civilization. But there are fanatics who prefer and advocate Turkish and Chinese abstinence. They say that there is "death in the pot," and that taxation is calculated to repress its use and reduce intoxication. But if a "beer tax" was able to destroy drunkenness and secure universal sobriety, it still would not be true "that that which is best administered is best" (Jordan), you would say that this is the maxim of tyrants and prohibitionists. That the making of manhood is more than the making of total abstainers. That temperance, which is self-government and suitable adjustment, makes men strong to use all the products of human industry without abusing them, and it may be added that there are millions of human beings who are intemperate in water drinking; millions more in sugar eating, and that there is no "pot" on earth in which "death" may not be found by fools.

The conclusion is inevitable. The "land tax" conforms in all its details with the general law of human life, which makes for more and better life among men. And the tax on beer is robbery.[44]

INDUSTRIAL BUCCANEERS AND INDUSTRIAL FEUDALISM.

Now, we have seen that co-operation in production and distribution and co-partnership in the product and surplus created by co-operation are essentially complementary elements of the law of collective human life, and that in consequence of the intimate connection between land and labor the larger part of this surplus is taken by landlords in the form of rent. But a little consideration will show that only the larger part goes in that direction. With a few honorable exceptions where the employers of collective labor, besides paying wages, divide the profits with their workmen, all such employers take the collective surplus to themselves;[45] thus, in making a contract for building a house, the contractor makes an estimate of the cost. He estimates all kinds of labor at the market price, including his own services and risks, the costs of materials, the interest on the capital required to provide the tools, transportation, etc.; and, when every necessity has been estimated, he adds a percentage to the wages of every workman, which, in fact, is the surplus value of their collective industry. It is in this way that gigantic fortunes have been made in building railroads, public buildings, and public and private works of all kinds.

Thus the law of co-partnership is evaded, and the surplus of collective industry seized by capitalists and employers, who are the buccaneers of industry.[46] Considering the vast number and importance of establishments of collective labor it is no wonder that contractors, manufacturers and employers become millionaires; and is it any wonder that they seek to extend their control of laborers by the establishment of trusts? Social agreement calls this enterprise, business, superior ability to organize labor; but is it not a taking advantage of the ignorance of the laboring classes, who are taught to believe that wages are all they are entitled to, and that they have no part in the product of their combined exertion?[47] Is it not, in fact, robbery?[48] Robbery of the same fund which goes to the landlord grabbing mill? The robbery of that wealth which individuals cannot create by their individual exertion, but which is a necessary outcome of their collective industry.

Now, experiment proves that co-partnership and co-operation make for more and better life among men.[49] There are to-day in Great Britain seven millions of its population, more or less, engaged in co-operation and co-partnership. A picked seventh of the population doing a business, manufacturing included, of 272 millions of dollars a year, with a bank of their own with deposits of sixteen (16) millions, and turning over two hundred millions (200,000,000) in trade. Many years ago I heard Robert Owen lecture on industrial co-operation and co-partnership; his first attempt was a grievous failure, but he was followed by Holyoake, Kingsley, Maurice, Tom Hughes, Vansittart Neal, Ripon, Ludlow, Godin and Leclair, and to-day there is scarcely a town in England without a co-operative store for distribution; and some of the largest and finest factories there and in the world are now owned and managed exclusively by working men, in the interest of the working men employed. For further evidence I would refer you to the recently published account of Labor Co-partnership, by Mr. Henry Demorest Lloyd, who says, "that industrial democracy can become a fact whenever the people will it."[50] The desire for property is universal, and the aptitude to manage it like "honor and fame from no conditions rise." Property, business and capital will never be properly managed until the entire people have a share in management, ownership and results.

From this it is evident that the law which applies to government applies to collective industry, viz., that no individual action can, by any possibility, replace the concerted action of the people (Jordan). Nor is the moral effect of co-operation and co-partnership less remarkable. Ralahine was a farm in the midst of one of the most turbulent districts in Ireland, where the people were ragged, hungry, lawless, and the lives of landlord and steward were in deadly peril. The owner was compelled to fly, and he left his estate in the hands of Mr. E. T. Craig, who explained to the laborers that henceforth they were to be their own masters; divide the work amongst themselves, and all share in the produce. The very ringleaders of previous disorder became the best workers. A commercial system of life was adopted; the people went into associated homes. They worked well and successfully. A co-operative store was opened, and labor notes were issued in the place of money. In three years the people became wonderfully changed. They left off drinking; they kept their homes clean; they paid the rent; disorder and violence ceased, intemperance became almost unknown. All had earned more than was paid by neighboring farmers, and the incident which was terminated by the bankruptcy of the proprietor remains a splendid illustration of what can be accomplished when the principle of brotherhood is appealed to.

Although I most strenuously object to the position that a question of justice is only truly determined by results, I can have no objection to inquire if the single tax "has been tried, if it works, and if its results on individual and social development are better than those attained through other forms of land tenure or of taxation," and the less because the comparison is with forms which have utterly failed to secure good results, and which no one pretends are founded on the principle of justice between man and man.

Now, it must be freely admitted that although the Single Tax was clearly promulgated by the French Physiocrats more than one hundred years ago, it has never yet been adopted in its entirety by any nation. On close examination, however, we shall find much evidence that its principle pervades many customs and much legislation, and that in so far it has produced the best results. As the cardinal principle of the Single Tax lies in rent and its distribution, it will be desirable to examine the various methods of dealing with rent, contrasting the effects upon the welfare of individuals and the community at large.

First, we have landlords pure and simple, en-

dowed with all the privileges of private ownership, who take all the rent, choose their tenants,
and discharge them when they please. They have
power to take all the traffic will bear, leaving the
tenant nothing but a bare subsistence, and in
special cases not even that.

The evil results of this limited rent distribution
are seen in Ireland. It is unnecessary to describe
the frightful condition to which the Irish people
were reduced about fifty years ago. Thousands
died of starvation and disease, while millions were
evicted from their miserable shanties and forced to
emigrate. At length the conditions became so in-
tolerable that a parliament of landlords was compelled to interfere, and to establish the inalienable
right of the inhabitants to live upon their native
soil before anything was paid to landlords. The
power to evict was taken from them, and under
the operation of the courts rents have been reduced more than one half, and the re-distribution
of rent has greatly improved the condition of the
people. The Irish are to-day more prosperous and
more contented than for centuries.

In the next place, all the privileges of full
ownership may be exercised by corporations.
These may be even worse than landlords because
they are totally devoid of human sympathy. But
when corporations are municipal and manage pub-

lic property, the rents are applied to provide for city needs.

In Freudenstadt, a town of 1500 inhabitants, there is no taxation. The public revenue is derived from royalties, rents, and other natural sources of wealth attaching to the town and neighborhood. The revenue has always exceeded the expenditure. There are neither paupers in the community nor unemployed. On one occasion recently there was divided among the inhabitants men, women and children, a sum amounting to $13.55 per capita. In England many municipal corporations either inherit it or have acquired land in the center of their cities. Old buildings have been torn down, new streets have been constructed, and the land rented out on lease. In a few years the rents of such properties will relieve the citizens of much taxation.

In the next place, the relation between owner and occupier may be determined by custom or by law, as under the feudal system, under which the relation between lord and villein was definitely fixed, if not always faithfully kept. As the lord acknowledged his fealty to the king by personal service or the presentation of a pair of spurs, so the villein secured the protection of his lord by so many days of personal service or so much produce, and, having rendered his dues with punctuality, he was left in peaceful occupation of his holding, and undisturbed possession of any surplus products which he might thereafter raise by his own industry. Thorold Rogers has fully described the comfortable and happy condition of the English peasants before the introduction of landlordism, and the frightful economic pressure which immediately ensued. The land then, for the first time in England, was treated as private property, and the occupiers were evicted because they were unable to pay interest on the purchase money. The Hon. Joseph Leggett has shown that the same causes have produced similar results in California. For the first twenty-five years after the first settlement land was open, and, except in cities, was cheap. The pressure of rent was very little felt, land was abundant, and the people few and contented. But when all the productive land was taken up, some for profit, more for speculation, rents began to rise and wages fall, for while landlords exist laborers cannot appropriate both. Then economic pressure began to appear, the rich became richer, and the poor poorer. Then appeared armies of tramps and thieves, and the independence of thousands was destroyed.

In the next place, the multiplication of individual owners results in diffusion of the rent, and has chiefly occurred in France, through the operation of the code of Napoleon; but the benefits of rent diffusion are obscured and neutralized by excessive military service and heavy industrial taxation. Nevertheless, one remarkable result has been attained; the food production of France has increased in the last century fifteen times faster than the growth of population, a practical proof that the so-called law of Malthus is not absolute.

In the next place, permanent occupiers may also be part owners, portions of rent being assigned to other persons on definite terms fixed by law. This form of land tenure has been in operation in the Channel Islands for a thousand years. The island of Jersey has never been subject to the Roman law, and therefore, there are still no landlords. The escape from landlordism was probably due to the poverty of the soil, which, until lately, was not able to support the inhabitants, much less to yield a surplus for the payment of rent. In the seventeenth century, as may be seen from the first edition of Falle's Jersey (1694), the island did not produce the quantity of food required by the inhabitants, who were supplied from England in time of peace, and from Dantzig in time of war. In the groans of the inhabitants of Jersey we find the same complaint. And Quale, in 1812, stated that the quantity of food was quite inadequate to their sustenance, apart from the English garrison.

After making, says he, all allowances, the truth must be told, the grain crops are foul, in some instances execrably so. We learn also from recent writers that the soil is by no means rich. It is a decomposed granite, without organic matter, besides what man has put into it. There are also seventy acres of an Arabian desert of sands and hillocks, with very poor soil on the north and west of it. Nor is the climate as favorable as might have been expected. There is an absence of sun-heat in summer, a remarkable prevalence of Jersey fogs, bringing mildew and blight in autumn, and much dry, cold, east wind, retarding vegetation in spring.

Land in Jersey has been held for centuries in small lots of a few acres. In the whole island there are not more than six farms of more than twenty-five acres, and upon these the celebrated Jersey cows are raised. The owner of the lot is permitted by law and custom to issue "rents" to the extent of three-fourths of the value of the holding. These "rents" represent a small proportion of the crop of wheat as raised a thousand years ago, when the soil was even more barren than at the beginning of this century, and the art of agriculture was much less advanced. So faithfully has this custom been preserved that the money payment equivalent to that small modicum of wheat secures to the occupier permanence of occupation. The possession of land is therefore absolutely safe to every cultivator, and cannot easily be alienated. To seize land for debt is accompanied with so many difficulties that it is seldom resorted to. The part owner and occupier cannot be compelled, as in the case of mortgage, to refund the principal. The laws of inheritance are also such as to preserve the homestead to the children, notwithstanding all or any debts the father may have incurred before his death. Custom provides also that the purchaser for cultivation undertakes to pay only a capitalized one-fourth of the total rent, and he often pays less; people are thus able to buy land for cultivation with very little capital, and the cost of conveyance is almost nothing. As there are no landlords on the island, there is no one to watch the crops, or raise the rent, no one to fix the terms of lease, no one to dictate the course of cropping, no one to raise the rent as population grows, every tiller of the soil is his own master, and occupies his little holding without interference from any one. While every occupier is an independent owner there are hundreds of other citizens who have an interest in rent, but without power to distrain for non-payment of the principal. Here then we have a clear recognition of the principle that rent belongs to the people, and a rough and unscientific method of distributing it among the population. In fact, the Norman custom is an imperfect Single Tax.

Other common privileges have also been carefully preserved. Every one is at liberty to gather seaweed for manure at a certain season of the year, and to dig sand at a distance of sixty feet from high water-mark.

And now let us notice the result. The island is eight miles long and less than six miles wide; it comprises 28,707 acres, rocks included. There are 1300 inhabitants to the square mile, or two to every acre, and, besides providing their own food, they now annually export $250 worth of produce from every cultivated acre. In 1894 they exported 60,605 tons of potatoes, grown on 7,007 acres, and for these they received about $2,300,000. They also exported 1600 head of cattle, chiefly cows, bulls and horses, and many tons of tomatoes, pears, salads and other produce. This success is entirely due to the amount of labor which a dense population is putting on the land. The fertility of the soil has been created by the industry of the inhabitants; it has been fertilized not only by sand and seaweed but with refuse of all kinds, inclusive of animal manures, city waste, stable manure, bones shipped from Plevna, and mummies of cats from Egypt. The ground is artificially warmed by the application of fermenting matters, and hot water pipes. An artificial climate has been created by the construction of acres of glass roofing, and the growth of the crops is promoted by the scientific manufacture of soils, the careful selection of seeds, and frequent replanting of the plants. These people realize the fact that it is easier and more profitable to raise ten tons of potatoes from three acres than it is from thirty. As there are no landlords the whole of the profit is distributed among the producers and the large number of persons interested in rent. It would be strange, indeed, if the Jersey islanders, densely crowded as they are, were not among the happiest, most prosperous, and most contented people in the world, which is the conclusion of every one who visits them. There is no poverty, except that which is personally produced; no pauperism; no unemployed; very little dishonesty or crime.

Here then we have positive proof that economic pressure is caused by landlords, and that it will be relieved by the Single Tax.

And now turn to cases where the tax on land values has been recently imposed. In New Zealand, the Legislature of 1891 imposed a graduated tax on land values, the lowest being .04 per cent. For twenty years previously the country passed through a period of fearful commercial depression.

It was overwhelmingly in debt, and the population was decreasing at the rate of twenty thousand a year. After the adoption of this form of taxation prosperity immediately returned, population began to increase, and the annual increase is now greater than the annual decrease before the passage of the act. United States Consul Connolly says of New Zealand, that it is now the most progressive country upon earth. That the private wealth of the people has increased over forty per cent., which is double the increase of population.

After five years' experience the New Zealand government extended the method of taxation to those municipalities which should choose it in preference to the older plan. Twenty municipalities have voted in its favor, and it is remarkable that the reform has been carried by the vote of property owners, and not by equal suffrage.

In 1895, the Legislature of New South Wales, having been thoroughly convinced of the successful reforms in New Zealand, passed a law abolishing all taxation on personal property and improvements, and levying four milles on the dollar on land value instead. Prior to the passage of the law the financial condition of the country verged on bankruptcy, and the people suffered great privation. One-half of the land was owned by less than one thousand people. 900,000 souls, men, women, and children, had not land enough in which to dig their graves. Immediately the large land speculators became alarmed. An English syndicate, which had acquired many thousand acres, put them on the market. Many large estates of 100,000 acres were readily disposed of in small lots, and in 1897 the increased area of land under cultivation was already 311,500 acres.

Landlordism still flourishes in the adjoining colony of Victoria, where the population is about the same, and where there is a high protective tariff. The contrast is convincing. In Victoria there are employed, in various trades, 37,779 males and 12,669 females. But in New South Wales there are employed 50,883 males, and only 6,689 females. For every ten ships docked and repaired in Victoria there are seventy in New South Wales. The deep sea ships in the Victoria harbors number between twenty and thirty, while in New South Wales they number between ninety · and one hundred. During a period of years, 5180 more men left Victoria than arrived, while New South Wales attracted 192,184 more than those who left. In New South Wales, both artisan and unskilled laborers are feeling the advantage of better times. The supply of workers is less than the demand, and the employee is the arbiter of his own compensation. In no other period has the value of imports been so great, its manufacturing output so large, and general prices and wages so satisfactory as during the two years just passed. The Premier said, on a recent occasion, small as the change has been, it has secured to the country for all time a good, sound principle of taxation, and it has killed the trade of the land gambler. In 1901 tariff on imports will entirely cease.

A most remarkable experiment with the Single Tax was made at Hyattsville, Md. In 1892 the town commissioners, believing they had power under the town charter, decided to assess land values only, so they abolished all taxation on improvements and personal property. In order to meet the loss of revenue the tax on land value was raised from fifteen to twenty-five cents on the hundred dollars. The effect was to reduce the taxation of householders forty-four per cent., and to raise the balance of sixty per cent. on land held for speculation and not for use. The effect was immediately beneficial; it lightened the burden of those most worthy of consideration. It promoted the improvement of property, the erection of new buildings and the employment of the people. There was no difficulty in the application of the system. The land speculators, however, set up violent opposition, and took the matter into the courts; and, it being declared unconstitutional, the town was compelled to return to the old system. All building immediately came to an end when the land speculators resumed their sway.

These results are all in favor of the Single Tax.

THE UNIVERSITIES AND THE LAW OF HUMAN LIFE.

It is the special function of universities to examine and illustrate those general laws which control the operations of the universe. To teach their order, correlation, beauty, adaptability to surrounding conditions, their sufficiency and perfection, their justice and morality, and to show how completely and surely they make for more and better life among men, whilst the least violation or neglect makes of necessity for starvation, misery and death.

Are the universities of America fulfilling their duties with respect to the law of human life? They seem ready and willing to acknowledge the value of intellectual and personal freedom, but have they put industrial freedom on an equal footing?[51] It would seem not; nay, rather are they not following the practices of the European universities of the last century? And just as those universities directed all their efforts to restrain intellectual and scientific freedom, so now those of America are using their great powers to strangle industrial freedom. None of these institutions, whose office is to extend the range of freedom, offer a protest against the artificial privilege of landlords. None are protesting against industrial feudalism, which is industrial tyranny. They have nothing to say on the absolute necessity of co-partnership in the results of collective labor as the only possible protection against the rapacity of governments, millionaires, trusts and corporations. They have failed to demonstrate the wickedness and folly of taxing individual industry as if it were a crime to work and create wealth.

They seem to sanction all those methods of taxation which bring lying and dishonesty in their train, and enable the rich to shift the burden on the poor. Common sense should tell them that all such methods make for starvation, misery and death, and that absolute obedience to the law of human life alone makes for more and better life among men.[52] In this, its first duty, the University of California, like those of America generally, is a grievous failure, and even Stanford, the most liberal, is by no means innocent.

It is significant that you should have so grievously misapprehended Mr. George's argument. That you should charge him with scientific ignorance possibly without having read his last great scientific work. That you should find his premises faulty and founded on figures of speech, when they are based on simple self-evident facts. That you should say that he takes out at the end only that which he puts in at the beginning, while in reality he puts in the beginning the simple facts of human life, and in justice between man and man takes out the Single Tax.

That you should regard his argument as not worth a straw's weight, whereas it involves the foundation of all human progress. It is no wonder that his last and greatest work on the "Science of Political Economy" is not in the Stanford library; and that the law of human life should be utterly ignored in the class-rooms, and is replaced by a study of the dreams of the French physiocrats of the last century; and this not for the purpose of picking out from all their writings those grains of wheat, the "produit net" and "impot unique," and of illustrating these grains of truth with the assistance of Mr. George's wisdom, but with the certain result that, without that wisdom, the students' intellects will be buried in the mass of chaff. And lastly, it seems to me incomprehensible that you should rely upon that inscrutable, uncertain, weak, mythical principle, "social agreement," as the authority for what is "right" when you have before you a simple law of nature which makes for more and better life among men, and the smallest neglect of which makes for starvation, misery and death.

It is painful to write these facts, but for you "truth" has no terrors, no humiliations, and it is necessary to probe to the bottom of the wound in order to effect a cure.

But this neglect of Mr. George's doctrine is the more remarkable at Stanford, because here, as always, interest is co-incident with obedience to natural law and duty. The Stanford estates suffer most grievously from the unjust system of taxation now in force, and from which there is but little hope of relief, except by the adoption of the "Single Tax," under which no rent can be taken from land in public use, of which the most important is the promotion of higher education. Rent taken away from such an institution is the worst form of robbery, and there is no possible excuse for it under the operation of the "Single Tax." It is true that the appropriation of land to public use is only a restoration of what belongs to the people, but this restoration was none the less a royal gift made by the founders of the Stanford University.[53] By it they renounced forever their artificial right as landlords, and gave back to the community that which the community had earned. But they did more, for they carried out the principle of the "Single Tax" to its uttermost point, and did, by the stroke of the pen, that which elsewhere must take many, many years to accomplish; and verily they shall have their reward, for the arrangement cannot be upset, and as the years roll by, and the population shall increase, the resources of the University are bound to grow in proportion to its need. What glory, what honor shall attach forever to such unselfish fulfillment of a general law as yet not recognized?

CONCLUSIONS.

In the foregoing I have endeavored to keep the main argument clear, short, and to the point. As Mr. George says, "We cannot if we would, we should not if we could, eschew the use of metaphor, but in questions of political economy it is necessary to base all metaphors on facts."[54]

I have shown that human life, happiness and progress depend upon the complete and faithful observance of the general law of independent and collective life. That this law is violated by the enactments and practices of social agreement, which cannot be accepted as an authority for "right."[55] That the violation of the general law of human life, even in the least particular, makes for starvation, misery and death. That the creation by social agreement of an artificial landlord class, endowed with power to deny "access to land," is destructive of industrial freedom, and that the appropriation of the product of collective industry by landlords, millionaires, trusts, corporations and individual employers is robbery. That co-operation in production and co-partnership in the collective result are essential elements of the law of collective human life. That the laborer to be really free must attain to self-employment as an individual, and self-government as a member of the collective body, sharing in the profits and management not as a favor but a right, sanctioned by the law of human life. That the taxation of individual industry is a violation of the law of individual freedom, and the final conclusion is that the "Single Tax" on land value, which is created by the collective activities and necessities of the whole community, is the source provided by the law of human life for the satisfaction of the common wants, no one being called upon to suffer loss individually on account of public need.

As under the "Single Tax" no one will care to have land except for possession and profitable use, millions of acres will be opened to the people. There will no longer be need to camp out for weeks upon the borders of land open to occupation. No longer need to fight and race and struggle for whereon to live, for *"free access"* will become a fact, and free materials will everywhere be found at the disposal of collective life.

Lastly, the law of independent and collective human life is the only complete and absolute basis of economics. It defines the origin of individual and collective wealth, and determines the rights of the respective owners in its distribution. It makes impossible the formation of trusts and combinations, which, under the pretense of better organization of capital and labor, and the promise of cheaper production, rob the producers of their individual and collective earnings. It gives the land and its natural resources to the whole people by the operation of the Single Tax, and thus destroys monopolies at their very roots; in fine, it makes for more and better life among men, and becomes a safe guide for statesmen, governments and professors of political economy throughout the world.

AN INDUSTRIAL UTOPIA.

You have wisely told your students that the Utopian element is one which our lives sorely need. That we have fought the devil long enough with fire. That we have attempted good results by evil means (social agreement, expediency, imperialism, landlords, trusts, bare subsistence wages, industrial taxation, licenses, franchises, and other special privileges, tariff and other inter-ferences with the law of independent human life); that unless our souls dwell in Utopia, life is not worth the keeping; that our windows should look toward Heaven, not the gutter. Now, with the help of the general law of human life it does not seem difficult to construct an industrial Utopia, which being the foundation of life is also the foun-dation of all human progress.[57] Let us suppose the creation of a huge industrial corporation to ex-ploit the earth. To become a shareholder it is only necessary to be a human being, endowed with intelligence and strength, who pledges his labor in return for life and the satisfaction of his wants. Every worker getting his wages according to the law of supply and demand, and those special con-ditions which determine the value of the service rendered. If but little service, bare subsistence; if more, comfort, leisure and the gratification of desires; if great, and rendered to the corporation, honor, glory, repose and luxury.

The charter of this corporation is the law of in-dependent and collective human life, as laid down in the foregoing pages. Every individual must be free to think, to act, and to assist in the business of the corporation, the exploitation of the earth, and be free to consume, hoard and dispose of his wages according to his will, whilst the surplus created by collective labor shall be gathered by the Single Tax, and distributed to the collective producers, not in personal dividends, but in provision for collective necessities and the gratification of collective desires.

The construction of the government of this corporation must be democratic.[58] That is, exactly that of a private business corporation. No individual action must be permitted to replace the concerted action of the people.

Nor need we forget that Utopia is beyond the reach of human action. That evil and death are as permanent as gravitation, and will forever remain essential elements of growth and progress. It is not our business if we never reach perfection. All men must be free to choose between good and evil, and we must be content with the rule of the majority. We may be assured, however, that the majority is for the most part right. and that our individual duty is to promote justice between man and man, and thus advance the brotherhood of all mankind. Now, I confidently claim your assistance in promoting this Utopian idea. It is exactly the form of government to which you were converted in relation to municipal affairs. It is the form of government adopted by business corporations and by English cities. I ask your assistance to teach it in your schools, that its operation may be extended to counties, States, and nations. This is "the ideal arrangement, although, perhaps, impossible. If it is impossible, it must become possible somehow before we can get on" (Jordan).

But nothing is impossible which is founded on truth, justice and natural law. Past experience proves it. One now can scarcely believe that only fifty years ago men were shot down and imprisoned for advocating vote by ballot and universal suffrage, and by honorable men, who believed their adoption to be impossible in England! Who could have anticipated the abolition of slavery in the United States fifty years ago? Even thirty years ago who could have dreamed that men would speak to each other a thousand miles apart? So, with or without the aid of universities, Industrial freedom must ultimately prevail, because it is founded on truth and justice and the law of human life. It is obedience to this law which constitutes true religion, and I would call upon the clergy of all denominations to adopt it as the basis of their teaching. This law provides the true remedy for ignorance, poverty, and immorality, and is the only safeguard against starvation, misery and death. This law promises the realization of that glorious document—the Declaration of Independence—which states so clearly that all men have equal right to life, liberty and the pursuit of happiness. This law which alone gives right to all men equally to gratify their physical and intellectual desires (Henry George). This law which is so well expressed in the motto of English co-partners "each for all, and all for each." This law which assuredly makes for more and better life among men (Jordan). This law which declares the equality of all men before natural law, and is the foundation of the brotherhood of all mankind.   STALLARD.

APPENDIX.

Note 1.—Adequate intelligence and adequate strength are not combined in the same man. (J.)

Men in general are neither idiots nor invalids. Man has nothing else to depend upon but intelligence and strength. (S.)

Note 2.—Labor is also exerted on labor or the past results of labor, also a form of industry. (J.)

Labor cannot be exerted on labor only. There can be no labor without land or its products. (S.)

Note 3.—Only by exchange. But one can be exchanged for another and must be in social cooperation. (J.)

But we are now discussing individual, independent life, and exchange is necessarily excluded from the argument. (S.)

Note 4.—Not in the tropics, nor when incentives are withdrawn by social force. (J.)

We are still discussing individual life, but even in the tropics food does not fall into his open mouth. He must also tramp and beg when social incentives are withdrawn. (S.)

Note 5.—But lacking intelligence, he begs this article; his slavery is endemic, not the result of force. (J.)

Nevertheless, many intelligent and highly educated men may and do become absolutely destitute, often the result of uncontrolable forces. Under present conditions they are compelled to beg for food or work. How many thousands have done so? How many masters of arts are cowboys in Texas? (S.)

Note 6.—Your argument that trees have not equal access to land seems to me without force.

(S.)

It is without force, but so is the statement that men have a divine or any other right to equal access. Trees, as individuals, are certainly dependent on access to land, men are not. (J.)

My statement is not that men have a divine or any other right to equal access to land, but a statement of simple fact, viz., that access to land is an essential condition in the maintenance of independent human life. Both men and trees exist on the conditions supplied by land, and would die without them. Equal access is simply an impossibility, and were it possible could not be maintained. This is nowhere proposed by Henry George. But the right or title of all men to access to land must be equal in order to secure to all men the possibility of living, and this equality is simple justice between man and man. Nor is it necessary that all men should be farmers, miners, or market gardeners to secure access to land, for it is obvious that access does not depend on the fact of occupation. The taking of rent affords an equal guarantee. Landlords have complete access to land by taking rent even when they are absentees. Rent is wealth created by the community at large, and by putting the community into the landlord's shoes every citizen gets access to land and shares both in the creation and expenditure of rent, no matter what his trade or occupation. Thus is simple justice between man and man secured by the operation of the single tax. (S.)

Note 7.—Trees are not endowed with intellect or active strength. (S.)

Neither are many men. Men must exchange one for the other. (J.)

Animals without intelligence or strength cannot be classed as men. Exchange is a necessity of collective, not of independent human life. Robinson Crusoe had no opportunity to make exchange until Friday came to him. (S.)

Note 8.—If all men depended on themselves for choice the world would be scantily populated. (J.)

There is no need for universal independence. Men gain too much from social intercourse and co-operation. (S.)

Note 9.—Once armed with the independent opportunity of maintaining life by the employment of his own labor upon land, a man, however destitute, is really free. (S.)

Not all. Robinson Crusoe could have suffered from almost any of the known forms of misery.

(J.)

True; but misery is not an essential condition of human life, and although a prisoner on the island, Crusoe exerted his intellect and strength on land and was made free to live. He was his own master. (S.)

Note 10.—He is no longer at the mercy of employers. (S.)

But he is at the mercy of brains. (J.)

While he has the independent opportunity of maintaining his own life by his own labor exerted upon land, he is at the mercy of nothing but superior force. Even then he remains master of himself. (S.)

Note 11.—If all men could get at the land, and could live when they got there, the earth would be too small to support them. There is much bad land, unproductive land, malarial land. Only the best tillage on good and healthy land, with brains in direction, will make civilized life. (J.)

This may or may not be true. But we are discussing the conditions of independent human life, not the progress of civilization or the future of the race. Nevertheless, the limit of production is not yet known. In East Flanders thirty thousand people live on thirty-seven thousand acres, all taken, and besides they manage to support 10,720 head of horned cattle, 3,800 sheep, 1815 horses, 6,550 swine, and to export flax and other agricultural produce. In one hundred years the food production of France has increased fifteen times faster than the growth of population—a practical proof that the so-called law of Malthus is not infallible. (S.)

LAW AND JUSTICE.

Note 12.—The law of independent human life provides the only line of action which secures the independent existence of human beings. (S.)

There is no such line of action—most of all depends on the being, his health and heredity. The law of independent life does not follow from the observed facts. You use nowhere the inductive method except in a few illustrations. Your real argument rests on an invention like "similia similibus"; in other words, you are guided by an assumed divine law. never yet tried except in part, and which you have discovered through "a priori" reasoning. There is no law which says, "This ought to be 'thus and so,' but is not. There are many (a priori) schemes of human life. You overlook the fact that the great problems are psychological, physiological and ethical rather than economic. I respect truth. but not the "a priori" method of reaching for it. That yields truth sometimes, but gives no test by which we can tell truth from moonshine. "Scientific men," says Professor Brooks (and I endorse his statement), "repudiate the opinion that natural laws are 'rulers' and 'governors' over nature, and look with suspicion on all 'necessary' or 'universal' laws." Man has never found out such. Certainly such laws are not rulers. We must rule ourselves within the limits of our environment, which is made up of cause and following effects.

I deny that all known natural laws make for more and better life among men. There are laws of decay as well as laws of growth.

We have not reached a point where deductive argument can prove anything to be trusted in human conduct.

What justice is can only be found out by experiment and attained only by the slow growth which is possible under governmental forms. I know of no way of getting at justice through the application of universal laws, because no such laws can bring credentials.

If, as Dr. Warner says, putting air in private hands would yield a better supply on juster terms there is no divine reason why we should not turn the atmosphere over to an air company. (J.)

If the skies fall we shall catch larks, but in my premises there is no "if." It is simple fact that men are animals endowed with intelligence and strength, and by exerting that intelligence and strength on land they obtain food and maintain existence. These facts form an impregnable basis of inductive argument. But in order to show that ethics, psychology and heredity have nothing whatever to do with the simple maintenance of life I will put the question in a simpler form. Thus: Men are land animals, and fish are water animals. Human and fish life depend, respectively, on the conditions to be found in land and water. Now life, land, and water are here metaphors. They mean more than the simple words express, but they are convenient and necessary and save long descriptions of well known facts; and the facts are that men live on land, and fishes in the water. This is no invention of mine. There is here no baseless hypothesis like "similia similibus," no "a priori" reasoning, no assumed divine law (whatever that may mean), no reference whatever to the purposes of nature, and I simply state the self-evident facts that men are born and live on land and fishes in the water. These facts a child can understand and no philosopher can doubt.

Now, natural law is the constant relation between definite antecedent facts or conditions (causes) and definite consecutive results (effects). Under this definition, to live on land is a natural law of human life, and to live in water is a natural law of fish life. Exactly the same reasoning applies to material bodies. The mutual attraction between two of them constitutes the natural law of gravitation. No reasoning can get closer to the facts; it is induction pure and simple. If not, I give the question up. But the law of human life as it depends on land, and the law of fish life as it depends on water, is not the whole law of life any more than the mutual attraction of two bodies is the whole law of gravitation; for as in the one case the antecedent conditions and consecutive results are definitely modified by density and distance, so in the others are the laws of human and fish life definitely modified by the million different influences with which they come in contact. But the fundamental law in all three cases remains constant and intact. If fishes do not get at water they die; if men do not get at land they starve to death. And two material bodies, if not mutually attracted to each other, would remain separate. The maintenance of fish life, like that of human life, is, therefore, purely and simply a question of economics. The water must be open to the industry of fishes, just as land must be open to the industry of men, and under these natural conditions only life is safe. It is simply nonsense to speak of the psychological, ethical and hereditary problems of fishes as involved in the maintenance of fish life, and it is difficult to define the age when they begin to operate in man, but it is clear that they have no more to do with the simple maintenance of human life than they have with moonshine.

In this there is no intention to ignore the importance of psychology, ethics and heredity in the the development of individual character and social life, but we are discussing the simple question of maintaining human existence, which, obviously, must be settled on a firm basis before the others can be reached.

In the next place, the sequence of events which constitute the law of independent life distinctly points out many things which ought to be "thus and so," but are not. For example, all men ought to have enough to eat and drink, and for this all men ought to have access to land, but landlords have been given the control and ownership of land by an edict of social agreement in direct antagonism to this "ought to be" of human life.

And here it becomes necessary to differ from Professor Brooks, and apparently from you also, as to the importance and value of all natural laws. You deny that all such laws make for more and better life among men, and say truly that there are laws of decay as well as laws of growth. But these laws are complimentary, one to the other. There is no decay without growth, and no growth without decay. Neither is there death without life, nor life without death; and it is therefore needless to argue that decay and death make for more and better life among men, for both are essential to the law—they constitute no exception.

Nor can scientific men afford "to repudiate the opinion that natural laws are 'rulers' and 'governors' over nature, or look with suspicion on all 'necessary' and 'universal' laws. Man has never found out such."

But what more suitable metaphors or what safer standards can be used? When we say that the sun rules the day and the moon governs the night, no one supposes that they rule by edicts, susceptible to change, but we simply mean that there exists an ascertained sequence of particular events so definite, so sure, and so constant, that we are able to tell the minute of sunrise at any given place, or any given day, in any given year, in any given century. A suspected law is not a natural law—the sequences have not been ascertained. It is no law at all. It is a surmise or presumption only. If we cannot depend on natural law (ascertained sequences) for our rule of action, chaos is still here.

And if "we have not reached a point where deductive argument can prove anything to be trusted in human conduct," where are we? On what other ground is it possible to stand? How otherwise progress?

Every successful action of human life depends on faithful obedience to some natural law that is "ascertained sequences." Men eat and drink to live. They depend upon the earth for food and on the air for the oxygen they breathe. They walk upon their feet; they see with their eyes, hear with their ears, and think with their brains, when they have any. These and a thousand other laws are natural laws of life, the violation of any one of which makes for misery and death. Are not the professors of Stanford searching the earth for truth, that is, for "ascertained sequences," for the benefit of human conduct? Has the law of evolution no lessons for effective human action? Or, to take a concrete example, the widest and closest observation has firmly established the relationship between temperance and health, and there is no difficulty whatever in applying this universal law to influence our lives and happiness.

Nor is experiment needed to determine what is justice, for justice is an eternal and unalterable principle of action, the law of which is as well established as the law of gravitation. Justice is simply "the equality of all men before the law." But not equality before all sorts of law; not equality before unequal law; not equality before untruthful law; not equality before bench law; not equality before military law; not equality before United States law—in fine, not equality before any human made law whatever. But justice is the equality of all men before natural law, which is alone just and equal and the only law which, when free to all men, as it should be, provides a certain guarantee that life, liberty and happiness are within the reach of all men.

Justice, therefore, simply gives to all men equal title to the benefits of "ascertained sequences," or natural law. It is injustice which denies these benefits to any, and such denial is continually ordained by human legislation and carried out by force.

Justice entitles no man to the exclusive use of any benefits due to natural laws, and neither governments nor constitutions can confer on some exclusive title to natural benefits which belong equally to others. "I will accept nothing for myself," says W. Whitman, "which all may not have the counterpart of on equal terms." This alone is absolute fairness between man and man.

The credential of jusice is not difficult to find; it is exposed on the very surface of all just laws, and attested by the absence of special privileges. All men are equal before natural law, but the injustice of social agreement, in the form of American law, has conferred special privileges on landlords at the expense of other people.

Moreover, justice does not "depend on governmental forms, nor is it attained slowly by their aid." Government in any form or by any means is incapable of creating justice or even of securing its attainment, for the relation of "all men" to natural law is personal and sacred, and is determined, not by governmental forces, but by the man himself. All that governments can do is to disturb the equality of right, as when it confers on landlords the exclusive privilege of private ownership of land, whereby they are enabled to exclude other citizens from the very source of life. Justice as thus defined is the foundation of individual freedom, and it is the only safe guide of human conduct. It applies to "all men," both in the individual and collective sense. It is the cardinal principle of democratic government, and the only reasonable hope for peace and good will among individuals and nations.

It is thus proved that the Government of the United States is a fortress of injustice, in which the acknowledged right of all men to life, liberty and the pursuit of happiness is fettered and confined. You declare that the only government you recognize is that which establishes justice, never that which establishes injustice, and I therefore confidently call upon you to assist in the alteration of American law that justice may be permitted to prevail.

Human legislation cannot even foster justice. It can only interfere with it; for whenever governments attempt empirically to correct or exterminate personal misdoings the freedom of justice is destroyed and the evil is increased.

For men cannot be made just to one another, honest, sober, clean, polite or virtuous by any form of human legislation. These are and ever must be personal considerations—to be determined by personal associations and personal education. When I was a boy drunkenness was the test of English hospitality. A gentleman dishonored his host by walking home; he honored him by drinking his three bottles and falling insensible underneath the table. The poor man also measured his happiness by the same standard and got home from the fairs and junketings after lying in the ditch all night. All this time there were laws to punish drunkards, from which, as usual, the rich escaped, and by which the poor and ignorant were scourged. Amongst the rich this test of hospitality has long since passed away, without any legal interference; public opinion has declared such conduct a disgrace to the class, but the poor and ignorant continue their excesses in spite of governmental forces.

For natural law is the only real schoolmaster which teaches wisdom and shows up the folly of disobedience to its righteous teachings. It is the master force of progress. Civilization advances as fast as the fools learn wisdom or are killed off by the law of evolution. Nature is kind to her true disciples, but has no mercy for the fools. When a man drinks to excess over night he gets a warning headache in the morning. If he neglects this warning, his liver, brains and family surely suffer, and with further persistence in his evil-doing comes misery and death. But human stupidity presumes to improve on natural law. It taxes drink, enacts prohibition, and closes the saloons. It fines and imprisons the drunkard when caught by the police. It fears that the fool will get another headache; that he may ruin his family, or even kill himself with drink. Thus, whilst natural law would utterly destroy the fools, human edicts are issued to protect them from their folly and to preserve the breed. Swaddling clothes and leading strings are only fit for infants, but *men* must be made to realize the consequences of evil doing, each on his own account. Under the uninterrupted reign of natural law fools will be overwhelmed in their own folly and wise men will increase and multiply.

All that justice wants, therefore, is a fair field and no favor. It asks no direct help from governments and human edicts. It grows by its own inherent force. It is fostered by personal education and by personal association with the just. In all other respects it simply asks to be left religiously alone.

But justice demands the destruction of all special privileges and the recognition by governments of the title of all men equally to the benefits of natural laws; individuals and nations may then rest in calm assurance that the power of good must in the end prevail.

Now, it is the province of schools and universities to search out truth and justice, which are but different expressions of the same great law, for there is no truth in injustice, no injustice in truth. It is for the professors of political economy to teach all governments that the progress of truth and justice is beyond the scope of human legislation, and that it is for individuals to choose between the happiness of good and the misery of evil. As Moses told the Jews, "Behold, I have set before thee this day, life and good, death and evil."

Man's whole business upon earth is to search out natural laws, whether of truth and falsehood, justice and injustice, good and evil, life and death. The more we know of these laws, the more accurately we trace their action, the more faithfully we follow their teachings for good and their warnings against evil, the longer we shall live and the happier we must be, for all natural laws (ascertained sequences) make for more and better life among men.

Note 13.—Social agreement is impotent to provide either food or employment for all manknd.

(S.)

Human action in any form is important. (J.)

If humanity is really impotent to provide its own food by its own exertion, it is very badly fixed. But there are pretty good indications that we may struggle on a few more centuries without fear of starvation. The little State of California could easily provide for another hundred millions if cultivated like the Channel Islands. If only 60 per cent. of the land of California were cultivated on the same scale as those islands, there would be adequate support for one hundred and twenty millions, and she still might export much more produce than she does to-day. (S.)

Note 14.—It is not your democracy nor any other ocracy that makes your people contented. It is because you have very much land and very few people.—Carlyle. (J.)

Free land makes a free and contented people. California should be the freest and most contented on earth. Yet it is not half as contented as the Channel Islanders, who number thirteen hundred to the square mile, and have neither tramps nor paupers. (S.)

Note 15.—This is not the whole story. Giving anything pauperizes. England has not land enough to support all her people if all had land and none worked on the results of labor. (J.)

The whole story is not necessary. Some pauperism is self-induced, but much more is created by the mistakes of social agreement and the injustice established by governments. It is not true that the giving of anything pauperizes. The Jews give freely to their poor, but do not pauperize. The giving or receiving of anything is, in itself, neither dishonorable nor degrading. It is a complete delusion to suppose that England has not land enough to support her population. If the cultivable area of the United Kingdom were cultivated as the soil is cultivated on the average in Belgium there would be food for thirty-seven millions of people, and England might export food without ceasing to manufacture (Krapotkin). If the population of the United Kingdom came to be doubled, all that would be required for producing food for eighty millions would be to cultivate the soil as it is already cultivated on the best farms in England, Lombardy, or Flanders, and to utilize meadow lands, which are now almost unproductive, in the same way as in the neighborhood of the big cities of France (Krapotkin). In 1870 I visited the Breton farm at Romford. It cost the owner £40 an acre, and had been cultivated by the former tenant and his two sons, with the help of two horses. At the time of my visit thirty men and twenty-five horses were employed, besides a hundred women and children. The annual cost of cultivation was $175 an acre, and the produce sold for more than double. The irrigation farm at Aldershot cost the English Government twelve cents an acre. It now rents for $100 per acre annually.

It is the incubus of rent which strangles English agriculture. The industrial classes of England have to pay their landlords one billion dollars annually for the privilege of standing on English soil; and they have to pay nearly as much again in taxes. The Liberals are now proposing to transfer one-fifth of the rental of England to the public treasury, relieving industry annually to the tune of twenty millions of dollars. Relieved of this overwhelming burden, the industrial classes will get higher wages and at the same time be able to compete successfully with any industrial community on earth.

SOCIAL AGREEMENT.

Note 16.—Social agreement cannot successfully control the conditions of independent human life.

(S.)

This does not follow. Property is not a divine right; it is a creation of social agreement which is the resultant of social forces, psychological forces and human history. Social agreement is a fact, using that term for its statutes or conventional operations among men. No statesman can rise much above social agreement, which is the inevitable result of laws and conditions. Social agreement must approximate the best conditions if civilization progresses; it declines if intelligence and activity decline. It grows better as men grow wiser. Men cannot grasp at higher laws they have not the wisdom to understand. Social agreement, like the methods of farmers, varies with the wisdom of its units. It is pretty bad yet. Most farming is equally bad. (J.)

The conditions of independent human life are as fixed and unalterable as the law of gravitation, and cannot be amenable to human statutes or the conventional operations of men. By defying ascertained sequences (natural law), individuals may turn night into day, and will surely suffer for their folly. So also social agreement may defy justice and establish starvation, misery and death. It has already done so. For social agreement has no definite principle of action; it has no respect for either truth or justice. There are communities in which social agreement makes heroes of the most expert thieves and most successful burglars. The general who kills most Filipinos will be worshipped by social agreement in America to-day. Social agreement supports protection in one country and free trade in another; imperialism in one place and popular government in another. There is no folly or injustice for which this mythical and many headed monster is not made the scapegoat. Social agreement is the tool of wealth; it is the slave of power; it has an unreasoning reverence for vested interests, even when those interests are most unjust in their nature and most injurious to the majority of people. Social agreement is the stronghold of special privileges, all of which retard the progress of industrial freedom. It is social agreement which takes twenty millions annually from the industrial classes of San Francisco for the privilege of standing on its soil and more than half as much again for taxes. It is social agreement which enables a privileged few to live in idleness and luxury on the industry of other people. Your verdict that it is "pretty bad" gives me the greatest satisfaction, but I am the more surprised that you should prefer social agreement to Divinity as an authority for the "right to property," for Divinity includes the idea of ascertained sequences, or natural law. What possible "right" can be established by "pretty bad" authority? What possible title has a "pretty bad authority" to grant privileges to some men and deny the same to others? Social agreement cannot influence human action successfully until it respects justice between man and man. This must be the standard to which all statutes and conventional operations among men must be referred before adoption. I confidently claim your assistance and that of your professors to destroy "pretty bad" as an authority for "rights" of any kind, and to establish justice as the cardinal principle of social action in the United States. (S.)

Note 17.—The community must get at land, not necessarily all its individuals. (J.)

All men must get at land, for no one can find a footing in the clouds. All men must have access to land for food.

Men can enjoy universal access without being farmers, miners, or market gardeners (vide note 6).

(S.)

Note 18.—In collective labor, there is "invariably" a surplus produced by the co-operators in their corporate capacity. (S.)

Invariably? Some men are devoured by wages. Cost of production can be less than product only when the greatest wisdom exists. (J.)

Invariably. There is no exception. Land is a prime necessity of all co-operative industry. The mere presence of the workers creates land value, which is the source of rent. Rent is a first charge on co-operative industry, and the landlord takes his rent even when the employer, through lack of wisdom, is devoured by wages. The landlord is the true devourer both of employers and employed. He takes his toll on all the wealth that they create, come what may. (S.)

Note 19.—The surplus of collective industry is conserved in rent; consequently land value increases with population. (S.)

This is purely theoretical. The value of a place depends in part on the scramble for it. (J.)

And what is the scramble but the higgling of the market, that which determines the value of labor and all other things? When the scramblers are many, values rise; when they are few, they fall. The scramble represents the price buyers are willing to give for the satisfaction of their desire for land, and when the public are purchasers, the value of the land for public use. This is fact, not theory. (S.)

PROPERTY IN LAND.

Note 20.—Property in land is a creation of social agreement. The world cannot prevent the men who got hold of Greece from becoming Grecians. Once Grecians, they did not give the barbarians half a chance. Although free appropriation may have been bad policy, it binds us just the same. If it is bad policy, don't do it again. If a deed was given to the first settlers in San Francisco we, who have agreed to recognize this act, or sworn fealty to the American Constitution, must recognize that the land is now theirs. Certainly the title of owners having such deeds is better than that of others who have none. This may have been unwisdom, but it gives no man and no community moral or legal right to correct it, unless a community agrees upon a method of correction. The community can only deal honestly and legally by paying for what it takes. The land is now in the hands of innocent purchasers, who have exchanged products of labor for it on the guarantee of title by the Constitution. The question is one of action to-day, but George's proposal to tax ownership out of existence is confiscation, whether taken all at once or in a thousand years. All taxation is accomplished by force. (J.)

In the first place, as to the legal compact and the American Constitution. In giving deeds to land owners, the Constitution reserved the right of taxation. Real estate is taxed in every State, often by separate assessment. Nor has any limit ever been imposed on such taxation by the Constitution of the United States. There is no constitutional obstacle to the taxation of land value even to the extent proposed by Henry George, for government may have full right under conditions to claim the lives and property of all the citizens.

The question is simply one of justice.

Now, the arguments here advanced are exactly those employed by the slave-owners fifty years ago. They admitted that slavery was originally the creation of force, and that the white people acted like Grecians and did not give the colored races half a chance; that the institution was adopted by social agreement and the Constitution, which recognized the deeds of transfer and enacted laws for its maintenance, of which the fugitive slave law was a marked example. The ownership of slaves had the same sanction as the ownership of land. Less than forty years ago slaves were in the hands of innocent purchasers, who had exchanged products of labor for them on the guarantee of title by the Constitution, and they said that although it might have been unwisdom, no man and no community had a legal or a moral right to correct it, and that the community could only deal honestly and legally by paying for what it took. Even this right was frequently denied. They complained that emancipation was confiscation.

And yet President Lincoln never did a more complete act of justice than when he issued his proclamation giving emancipation to some millions of his fellow citizens, recognizing the fact that justice demands the equal application to all men of the ascertained sequences associated with human life, of which personal freedom is an essential element.

But if the destruction of land ownership be confiscation under the law of justice, what special claim have landlords for exemption over other people? Professors of political economy seem to think that confiscation only fits the rich. They never protest against the confiscation of the poor man's industry. The sacrifice of a man's labor, skill and subsistence, in fact, all that he has to live upon, is called the inevitable result of social progress, never confiscation, and no one proposes remuneration for the loss sustained. Then why should landlords be paid for what they never earned?

Forty years ago twenty thousand sober, industrious, working tailors in Whitechapel, London, were reduced to absolute starvation by the introduction of the sewing machine. To-day the linotype machines are taking bread out of the mouths of thousands of intelligent compositors, who have given the best part of their lives to the faithful service of the public, and now, being good for nothing else, they have been driven down to the bare subsistence scale of wages by conditions utterly beyond their own control. Why should not landlords, who have enjoyed so many comforts in the past, be made also to fall before the Juggernaut of human progress? The slave-owners fell, and why not landlords also?

But the sacrifice demanded is not all loss. The troubles anticipated by the slave-owners have not been realized or have had their compensation. They are no longer degraded by association with slavery, the separation of children from their parents and the cruel whip. They have been humanized and freed from responsibilities beyond their power to discharge, and to-day there is not to be found a slave-owner of forty years ago who would restore the institution.

And justice will be equally lenient to landlords, but few of whom will be reduced to common labor, as the use and occupation of their lands will remain secure and they will not be deprived of improvements henceforth to be relieved from unjust taxation.

Like the slave-owners, the landlords will be freed from an odious thraldom. They will cease to be the drones of social life. They will be saved the perjury and deception by which they now shamefully shift the burden of taxation on to the shoulders of the poor. In spite of themselves they will be made honest men. Deprived of rent, the pious thief will no longer be able to steal thirty millions annually from the earth, which is the public treasury of wealth, and he will no longer have need to bribe legislators or to establish professorships of political economy to promote, sustain and justify his robberies.

And as regards the recipients of justice. The serfs of industrial bondage have a decided advantage over the slaves of the past. Freedom was for them a new experience. They were too ignorant to take advantage of it. But, happily, the serfs of industry are not all reduced to the condition of "The Hoe" man, and even he would stand upright and have an upward look if his bondage were removed.

Now, the application of rent to the public service and the relief of every industry from taxation would create a new world, both for the producer and consumer. The rent of the oil fields would pay the war tax, and the rent of mines the current expenses of the government, and as rents decline, wages, being complementary thereto, would rise. Not a laborer in the United States but would be able to provide two or three suits of clothes where he now possesses one. The impulse given to commerce and manufactures would be irresistible. A home market would be created ten times greater than that of all China and the East. As Kropotkin says, "let your factories be employed, not in supplying the wants of enslaved Filipinos, but to satisfy the unsatisfied needs of millions of Americans." Over-production would become impossible.

Thus the quality of justice, like that of mercy, is not strained. Whether it comes like dew from heaven upon the earth beneath, or with war, fratricide and death, it still will come twice blessed. It blesseth him that gives and him that takes. The conclusion is clear. All rent is created by the activities and necessities of the people. It belongs to them, and in justice the landlord takes nothing but his share of public benefit. Justice has no half-way house. It never compromises. It may be denied its rights, but it never gives them up. It takes all that it can get, but is never satisfied until all special privileges are utterly destroyed. Governments, therefore, have the same legal and moral right to abolish private ownership of land as they had to abolish private ownership of slaves.

Nor is the emancipation of the serfs as hopeless now as was the emancipation of the slaves only fifty years ago. Men are beginning to grow wiser. The industrial classes are beginning to feel their bondage. They are commencing to realize that land is no man's property any more than air or sunshine. They see that the productiveness of land is enormously, nay, indefinitely, increased by human industry, and that justice and common sense alike demand that the occupation and use of land shall be as widely and equally distributed as possible amongst all mankind. They see that the single tax leaves the land itself intact, does not diminish production nor imperil permanence of occupation. It simply takes the rent for public use and destroys the privilege of private ownership.

Lastly, the single tax is not forcible taxation. Unlike the cyclone, which is violent, destructive and partial in its operation, the single tax acts like the silent, unfelt, beneficent pressure of the atmosphere. Industrial taxation operates only on special classes and passes by the landlords, who are protected by their rent. But the single tax operates universally on all. No one can possibly escape. No one can shirk his duty. No one can shift the burden on another's shoulders, and the pressure will not be felt, being equal in all directions and perfectly adjusted to the advantages received.

Now, in face of the certain fact that the landlords will lose their grip upon the ballot-box, which must soon become the impregnable fortress of human independence, and that producers and consumers number ten to one against their enemies, the landlords, there is not only hope but certainty of eventual victory. So, when the industrial classes come to know and have courage and independence to exercise their power, social agreement will be forced to change the statute, which is all we want. (S.)

Note 21.—The rise in land values was exceptional. California was treasure trove, and divided up by the law of bushwhackers. (J.)

In every city in the world land values have risen, ceteris paribus, in proportion to population and the necessities and activities of the people. They have increased more in Chicago than in San Francisco. San Francisco, in fact, presents an exception which supports the rule, for while population has increased during the last ten years land values have declined, because speculators had created a fictitious boom. (S.)

Note 22.—There are two sides to this picture. Public money which does not cost makes irresponsible waste. (J.)

There is no public money which does not cost brains, strength, and industry, and those who make it have the right to dispose of it at will. (S.)

Note 23.—A stable lease would permit development. A long lease has often been regarded as substantial ownership. It is therefore prohibited in California. (J.)

This is surely a condemnation of private ownership in any form. (S.)

Note 24.—Society cannot separate legally from rightfully. (J.)

The misfortune is that it does so all the time. Legally is human law, edicts, or ordinances; rightfully is ascertained sequences. Legally is unstable, one thing one day and something else the next; rightfully is permanent and unalterable. Legally is quite as often wrong as right; rightfully is always right. Civilization advances as the two approximate, and when they coalesce we will have nothing to complain of. (S.)

Note 25.—So do the weaker live upon the strong. If there were no weak, life would be easier for the strong. (J.)

The weak only exist, they do not live upon the strong, and the uniform result is that the few strong get stronger and the many weak get weaker. (S.)

Note 26.—Difficult problems, not to be solved on economic lines. (J.)

But cannot be solved on any other lines. because the economy of simple existence stands before every other consideration. (S.)

Note 27.—Not true. (J.)

Hunger is the chief cause of crime, drunkenness and ignorance. It is impossible to teach a hungry child or get effective labor out of a hungry man. Sufficient food is the one absolute condition of an independent life, and its provision is a question of economics (vide note 12). (S.)

Note 28.—Industrial bondage is one of the smallest factors in human misery. (J.)

It is the fundamental factor, because industrial freedom is the basis of economics and of independent life. (S.)

Note 29.—The law of wages tending to the bare subsistence point, called "natural" by Stuart Mill.

(S.)

It is natural, that is, the wage system so works.

(J.)

It is not natural, because the antecedents are neither constant nor necessary, nor are the results uniform. (S.)

Note 30.—All natural laws make for more and better life among men. (S.)

Certainly I deny this. There are laws of decay as well as of growth. (J.)

Vide note 12. (S.)

Note 31.—Who takes the wealth produced individually and collectively by the laboring classes? Are they not governments, landlords, millionaires, trusts and corporations? (S.)

Also idlers, beggars, paupers and unskilled laborers. (J.)

Yes, but the one obtain their wealth by means of special privilege and force, and the others cannot help themselves while social agreement denies them equal opportunity to earn their share by labor. (S.)

SOCIAL PROGRESS.

Note 32.—Yet in no land and at no time of the world was the condition less unfavorble. (J.)

On a superficial view this seems to be entirely true. Everywhere we recognize the marvelous growth of wealth and luxury, the numerous inventions of labor-saving machinery, the harnessing of natural forces to the service of mankind, the stupendous advance of Art and Science, the rapid construction of cities provided with all the conveniences and luxuries of modern life, the improvement of sanitation and the prolongation of human life; and last, but by no means least, the extension of education, especially in the higher branches.

But none of these are evidence that justice is increasing between man and man. They therefore afford no proof that the real condition of society is better now than it ever was before. Nor is the conclusion supported by any past experience, for whenever the power of a class has grown up under the fostering wing of special privilege, whenever wealth has accumulated in the hands of drones and non-producers, whenever land and its products have become the property of a comparatively few monopolists, poverty and dependence have invariably grown faster than the wealth and luxury. And not all the pomp of power, not all the forces of civilization have been able to stifle the fire of injustice and oppression raging underneath the surface, and no nation has been able to withstand the explosion which eventually took place. In spite then of all appearances, it may yet be true that the condition of society, even in this favored land, was never more unfavorable than it is to-day.

Neither wealth nor education can be regarded as tests of social progress. Andrew Carnegie says that it is certain that the men who do the work do not get rich. Wealth does not justly come to its producers. The rich become richer and the poor poorer. And education, without industrial freedom for its basis, only creates desires and ambitions more rapidly than the means for satisfaction. In that case men become discontented and are tempted to live by their superior wit on the industry of others rather than their own, which tends to robbery and crime. The decrease of in justice between man and man is the only measure of sound progress, and this is attested by the decrease of poverty and its consequences, which may be easily observed.

"To make men good and kind and noble, and to give them independence, it is necessary, first and foremost, to satisfy their material wants. When one's whole time and energy are needed to fight for the necessaries of life, there is no opportunity for the cultivation of those higher qualities which distinguish men from brutes. Poverty is not a genial soil for culture. Only the weeds of ignorance can thrive on it. There are no moral considerations in the presence of starvation; no intellectual needs while material wants remain unsatisfied." ("The Story of My Dictatorship.")

(Moreover, the worst forms of poverty do not appear upon the surface for "to be poor and seem poor" is repugnant to all men, especially to men of education, who therefore cover up their needs. Poverty may be best discovered by its inseparable associates, first, involuntary and unnatural indolence, the consequence of insufficient or unwholesome food, and bad environment, a form of indolence which soon becomes habitual and hereditary; then loss of self-respect and independence, then crime and immorality in every form.

To the needs of poverty and to the artificially-created needs of fashion equally imperative, women sacrifice their virtue, merchants their credit, educated men their honor, and all of them seek the use of artificial stimuli to raise their drooping spirits or to excite their exhausted bodies for more exertion. But once give men justice, once give them equal opportunity to take the benefits of natural law, which are more than sufficient for the satisfaction of their material needs, once banish poverty, and the fear of poverty, and human nature may be safely trusted for the rest.

But let us examine the question from a practical point of view, taking the City of San Francisco as a good example. Here, if any where, the progress of social organization may be definitely seen. For here we have the capital of a State, the richest in natural resources upon earth, whose mountains are loaded with gold and precious minerals, and whose valleys are so fertile that a hundred inhabitants could be sustained in comfort, where there is only one to-day. A city built upon the foreshore of one of the finest harbors in the world—the Golden Gate to the Pacific Ocean—the open doorway to the commerce of the Orient. To this glorious spot came a community selected by the law of evolution. Invalids died by thousands on the way, and dullards stayed at home. All men came with an equal chance. Lawyers, doctors, bankers, and divines worked side by side with miners, teamsters and common laborers; there was work and opportunity for all, and this active and intelligent community has been continually reinforced by men of energy and intelligence from every region upon earth.

There was much open land, and the incomers were few and contented. But we have seen that the city began with an unjust appropriation by a few individuals of all the land in sight, and when, after a quarter of a century, all the useful land in the State was similarly taken up, a change began, and, if the change has worked righteously and well, if the condition of society is really less unfavorable, we may reasonably expect, due allowance being made for the increase of population, that there is now less poverty, less crime, less immorality, less need of policemen, jails and alms houses, and proof beyond doubt that the condition of the mass of citizens is becoming less and less unfavorable every year.

Now, in 1874 the millionaires were few in number, but have since then steadily increased. No one has lived in the City during the last quarter of a century can doubt that the few rich have become richer, and as they have long since ceased to be producers, their wealth has accumulated at the expense of other people. They have taken toll of the collective industry of their fellow citizens in the shape of rent, and to-day the industrial classes of San Francisco pay the landlords twenty millions annually before they get a bite of food for themselves and families.

Forty per cent. of the municipal and State taxation is also paid directly by the industrial classes, besides poll tax and their contribution to real estate taxation making up the whole. Besides this they pay the larger portion of Federal taxation, all of which is paid by the consumers. Under these conditions poverty cannot possibly diminish. The landlords take the cream, and leave to the rest skim milk.

And now examine the return of crime. The following figures are taken from the Municipal Reports:

	1874.	1898.	Increase percent.
Population	200,770	360,000	79
Number of Police	121	559	362
Arrests by Police.........	13,000	29,168	112
" of Drunkards	5,092	12,738	150
" for Burglary.......	124	274	121
" for Grand Larceny..	149	290	94
Divorce Suits	428	911	112
Suicides	56	146	160
Inmates of Alms House....	340	912	168
Inmates of State Prison...	931	2,207	127

Every one of these items affords indisputable evidence of increasing poverty, and every one indicates that the condition of society is steadily growing worse notwithstanding the increase of wealth and knowledge, and the advance of education.

This conclusion is also supported by strong individual testimony. The Rev. Father McDonnel writes: "I am by no means a pessimist, but for fifteen years I have lived among the poor, and talked and felt with them. I cannot find one person to deny that the industrial conditions were not more favorable in 1874 than in 1899. It is now much more difficult to obtain employment, wages have steadily declined, and are going down every year. The reduction of prices of necessaries and luxuries is not in the same proportion. The working classes are certainly more dissatisfied with their condition now than ever before in the history of the world. This dissatisfaction is growing yearly. Cases of involuntary destitution are very frequent. I have known cases of voluntary death by starvation, and I should say that want of employment is often a cause of suicide."

Mr. Fitzgerald, for many years connected with the laboring class, and now State Labor Commissioner, says: "The strongest evidence of the increasing economic pressure is the invasion of women into nearly every employment, for women only go to the workshops as a last resource. In my experience, I have found employment for 18,000 workers, and I can say with truth that there is no position so hard and laborious, no hours so long, and no wages so poor and insufficient, which I could not fill in forty-eight hours' notice, provided food and shelter were included. Only a few years ago the coalworkers of Pennsylvania offered to contract their services for life, if the mine owners would engage to provide them with the necessaries of life. According to my experience economic pressure is increasing every day."

To this important testimony let me add my own: In 1874 I was staying in the country, and was introduced to "the lady" who condescended to do my laundry at 25c. a piece. In the same year in the city, we all paid invalids 25c. for cleaning boots, a service now rendered by able-bodied men for 5c., and there are hundreds of competitors at that. The invalids are now either begging in the streets or have been driven to the Alms House. Unlike military pressure, economic pressure takes away the weak. In 1874 the wages of farm hands were $30 a month with board and lodging in the winter, and $60 in the summer. Now they are $5 a month in the winter, and from $15 to $20 in the summer, and there still remains an army of tramps, and involutary disemployed. In 1874 country people never locked their doors; to-day none but the foolish leave them open. In 1874 the number of defaulting bankers and municipal officials were not comparable with the same to-day. The number of "misfits" seems to be steadily increasing in every profession. In 1874 I had no difficulty in collecting fees from even the poorer classes; now the rush to hospitals and polyclinics for gratuitous advice is overwhelming.

But, after all, what is the truest test of the economic condition of the body politic? Surely, that it secures the existence and reasonable comfort of all its members; and the question is, do intelligent, able and industrious people ever succumb to involuntary destitution? Most certainly they do. In San Francisco such deaths are increasing in number every year out of all proportion to the increase of population.

Let me give an illustrationn: In January last Mr. and Mrs. T. arrived in San Francisco with two young children. He was sober, steady, industrious, and had been prosperous. He failed to obtain employment, but his wife secured work as a seamstress. Her earnings, however, were insufficient for the family support, and she denied herself necessary food. After 16 hours' work, without food, she went to her husband, and exclaimed: "Oh! the pain of it. I am fainting; dying for want of food"; and sinking on the floor she was picked up dead. There is here no evidence of hereditary taint, no evidence of ignorance—a case which neither charity nor poor laws can provide for or prevent. A case due to economic conditions unfavorable to the maintenance of life, conditions absolutely destructive of personal independence; conditions created by society itself, and which become worse and worse the longer they exist and the more perfectly they are carried out.

But in San Francisco to-day there is direct evidence of a still more pitiable poverty—more unbearable than any which has before presented itself in any land or in any time of human history, for men and women are driven almost daily to a voluntary self-inflicted death by inability to obtain employment. They prefer suicide to dependence on others—sure evidence that they are neither ignorant nor idle. Let me give some illustrations which have occurred during the last few months:

R. R., Aet 42, had a wife and two children. He was a hard working, industrious and sober man. He took whatever work offered and was able to support his wife and family. Work becoming scarce, destitution stared him in the face, and he hanged himself.

E. H. W., Aet 60, a foundryman, unable to obtain work, hanged himself.

Miss G., Aet 50, a nurse of experience and good character, not obtaining work, and being requested to vacate her lodgings, hanged herself.

F. I., Aet 45, a laborer, unable to find employment, jumped into the bay. When rescued he declined to state whether he would make another attempt to end his life.

G. W. R. came to San Francisco at the beginning of the year in search of work. He brought several credentials as a steady man, attentive to his duties and entirely satisfactory to his employers. He wrote an excellent hand and was fairly educated. He kept a diary. On February 11th he went to work cutting timber. After a week he was seized with chills and fever and had to quit. He rode on the train a little way and then walked. He slept in a shanty and walked to Albion next day, "but it was a hard pull over the mountains." Next day tried to walk to Point Arenas, but had to stop five miles from it; too tired to go any further. Slept in a barn. February 24, arrived at Point Arenas at 11:30. Got dinner, most awful hungry. February 27, arrived in San Francisco at 3 a. m.; remained on board boat till 7 a. m.

Went to S. V. W. W. for work. No go.

March 1. Found nothing yet.

March 2. Nothing without money to pay for it.

March 3. No chance of getting anything to do. What will I do? No money, no friends, no work. Sick with heart trouble. God help me.

March 7. Cannot find anything to do yet.

March 8. Am living on doughnuts; 5 cents a day. I don't know where to go or what to do.

March 9. My last quarter gone for room rent.

March 10. God help me; have only 5 cents left. Can get nothing to do. What next—starvation or ——

March 11. Went to see about two places this morning the first thing, but had a chill at the time, so could not get it. Sick all day; this morning chill, and burning fever in the afternoon. Nothing to eat to-day, since yesterday morning. I'll have to starve or die now.

And he carefully stuffed up the keyhole and turned on the gas.

How one must admire the courage of the man. Hungry, chilled and feverish from want of food, one meal in many days, he nevertheless presents himself for work, hoping to the last.

Now, I confidently defy the production of any such cases among the four and a half millions of inhabitants of London. In all my experience in the early forties, when in my native town, twenty per cent. of the people lived on public charity, where I have seen hundreds die from starvation, the result of economic pressure, I never saw a suicide death to escape that pressure. In the slums of Whitechapel, Bethnal Green and Holborn, where I was for some years a guardian of the poor, I never saw suicide as the result of destitution, and yet within the last few months in San Francisco, where the citizens spent a quarter of a million for ten days' opera, such suicides are of constant occurrence. They form a large proportion of the enormous increase of suicides of the last few years. It is not the death chosen by thieves and paupers and the dependent classes, but the death of intelligent, self-respecting men driven to desperation by the inexorable conditions of society, in which justice has no place. My conclusion is that in spite of all appearances the economic condition of the mass of the people was never less unfavorable than it is to-day.

Note 33.—Sufficient education, wisdom and thought frees any man. (J.)

Not without sufficient food. (S.)

Note 34.—This is true. But he added no new facts, and no new deductions. He advanced our knowledge of economics in no appreciable degree.

(J.)

Henry George never claimed originality. But he has revolutionized the science of political economy. He has fully and successfully exposed the fallacies, confusions, and want of scientific accuracy to be found in all accepted treatises and textbooks, particularly with regard to wealth, value, etc. For the first time a distinction has been accurately made between human and natural law, the one being the mutable will of man, the other the immutable will of God. He has shown that true science deals only with natural laws, and that with human laws, except as furnishing illustrations and subjects for investigation, the science of political economy has nothing whatever to do; that it is the science of the maintenance and nutriment of the body politic, that is, of man's relation to the earth.

That this relation is independent of moral, ethical and political considerations, and that the due adjustment of their relation lies at the foundation of all scientific economics and social progress. He shows that the facts and conditions of this relationship constitute a series of definite sequences which we describe as natural law, and this natural law is the only true basis of economics ever promulgated.

His "divine authority" is simply metaphor for "natural law" or ascertained sequences, and his moral law simply justice between man and man. Thus, political economy has been taken from "the dreamy and indefinite" and established for the first time on a scientific basis. This service is alone sufficient to place Henry George amongst the most distinguished scientists of modern times.

(S.)

Note 35.—And so has Christian science, homeopathy, vegetarianism, transubstantiation. All that brings healing, happiness or the millenium in some way easier than your way or mine. (J.)

Proof that results must always be corrected by deductive reasoning from the sequences of natural law. (S.)

Note 36.—I do not doubt the wisdom of taxing unearned increment rather than industry; but I do not think that George's method of argument has added anything permanent. He was a preacher, and his converts, when they are numerous enough to try his experiments, will demonstrate its good and evil results. (J.)

I submit respectfully that George's argument of divine authority, which in fact is natural law, is at least as good and more reliable than the argument from social agreement, which is human law. Anyway, I am delighted that you acknowledge the wisdom of taxing unearned increment rather than industry. I have also little doubt that with further thought you will realize the crass folly of taxing any form of industry, as if there could be too much wealth created. Even now I may say truly that thou art almost persuaded to be a single taxer.

Note 37.—I do not refer to the tax on land value in these words, but to the argument drawn from divine intention in their interest. (J.)

Is not this a quibble about words? Divine authority and the purposes of nature are simply indefinite metaphors, intended to express natural law, just as natural law is metaphor representing definite sequences of particular events. (S.)

Note 38.—Instead of "general law," put facts and conditions in the community or race in question. (J.)

In no community or race would facts or conditions provide reliable wisdom or a sure guide for action.

Note 39.—No "law" makes for anything else than cosmic order. (J.)

Ascertained sequences undoubtedly make for cosmic order. The "law" of human life is an example or the law of gravitation. But human "law" continually makes for cosmic disorder. The bare subsistence "law" of wages is a good example, and makes for starvation, misery and death. (S.)

Note 40.—Why not? What are taxes for? To improve land? (J.)

Taxes are imposed to satisfy social wants. If there is no society, there are no social wants and no taxation. Until a man becomes a citizen his land has no value. There is no market, no higgling. His industrial products are all his own And on the principle of justice are free from taxation for the benefit of other people.

Note 41.—It expands, but not necessarily in proportion. (J.)

"Cateris paribus" and practically in exact proportion. (S.)

Note 42.—The single tax would not be adequate in mountain districts to make them inhabitable.

(J.)

They would remain deserted until a mine was found. (S.)

Note 43.—Who made that law? It is desirable, but not a "law." (J.)

It is the "law" of justice which secures to every laborer the absolute possession and disposal of the product of his own exertion. (S.)

Note 44.—It is not robbery if agreed to by the parties concerned. It may or may not be wise, that is a question of fact. But one is no more divine and no more robbery than the other. (J.)

But the consent must be intelligently and voluntarily given, with adequate compensation. To take from people who are asleep or ignorant of their just rights only aggravates the robbery. Stanford improvements are unjustly taxed, in spite of the protest of the Trustees, and the tax is paid under duress of human edict, which does not make it just. The tax on land value you acknowledge to be wise, and this is so because it is established on the principle of justice between man and man. But the tax on beer taxes one man for the privilege of drinking beer, whilst by so much other citizens are relieved of taxation. This distinctly is not equal treatment, and therefore is not justice. In straight English, it is nothing less than robbery. If justice is divine, the tax on land value is also divine, but avowedly the tax on beer is not.

(S.)

Note 45.—Because they suffer all collective losses. (J.)

No. They charge insurance against loss and put it in the contract. (S.)

Note 46.—Capitalists are the bucaneers of industry. (S.)

And also its makers. Laborers do not make the conditions under which they work. (J.)

Capital promotes but does not make industry, but industry alone makes capital. Employers and employed both work under the conditions given them. (S.)

Note 47.—This is true only in part. Unless wisely controlled, collective labor cannot produce wealth. (J.)

Very little wealth can be produced without it. (S.)

Note 48.—No, it is not robbery until we can legally forbid it by devising something better. (J.)

If taken unjustly, it is robbery if we had twenty other plans. The collective co-partnership is hopelessly handicapped by the privileges of landlords and capitalists, who take all the traffic will bear.
(S.)

Note 49.—When men are wise enough to co-operate intelligently, they can free themselves from the cost of control. (J.)

They will. (S.)

Note 50.—They will it as they fit themselves for it. (J.)

And the opportunity will make them fit. (S.)

Note 51.—Industrial freedom must be individual and personal. (J.)

It must also be collective and general. That which is true of "all men" as individuals, must also be true of "all men" collectively. All freedom is individual and personal, whether intellectual, industrial or political. This is all I contend for. (S.)

Note 52.—Universities are only places for investigation. They utter no protests as universities. But every fact is investigated, one as impartially as the other. For "a priori" theories investigators care nothing. Economists have studied carefully all methods of taxation possible and impossible, with no more prejudice than you have, each with such power as was given him to search out truth. That they regard the "Single Tax" as at best a choice of evils, is because no facts have taught them the reverse. All this is matter of opinion. Stanford stands for the search of truth. It has engaged the ablest economists it could find and pay for. Of these, Dr. Warner was pre-eminent in all matters he touched. Ross and Durand are not bigots, nor does any influence check their freedom of thought and speech. (J.)

Admitting that universities are only places for investigation, and that they utter no protests as universities, all that can be reasonably expected is, that their investigations shall be impartial, and the results declared and advocated consistently with truth and justice. But scientific investigators do not ignore hypothesis, for without its help scientific progress would be extremely slow, and with its help some of the grandest results have been obtained. If the law of independent and collective human life were nothing but hypothesis, which is not true, it might still be worth serious consideration, and might lead to magnificent practical results, particularly as the present condition of society is by no means satisfactory.

But to declare that (economic) facts are investigated with impartiality, and that economists have carefully studied all methods of taxation, possible and impossible, without prejudice, each with such power as was given him to search out truth, seems to me impossible. For are not many of the Universities of America founded by Landlords, Monopolists, and Millionaires, who make the professors possible, and pay their salaries? Are not all American professors supported by the spoils and robberies of the landlord system and by unjust taxation? How shall professors so placed be expected to kill the goose which lays the golden eggs? Fancy a professor, created and supported by a Rockefeller, turning round and telling his patron that he was going to teach the students economic justice under the operation of the Single Tax, and that Mr. Rockefeller has no more title to the oil he steals from the public treasury of wealth than the most miserable infant born in the slums of New York. How could he say that he would tell his students how to destroy land ownership, how to put an end to unjust monoplies, how to distribute natural benefits more equally among the people, and prevent all future public robberies?

Professors appointed under such conditions accept the collar of the millionaire. Their province is to bolster up the actions of their patron and to invent specious arguments against the justice of the public claim. If the benefits of land occupation belong in justice to the people as a whole, it is the people who will have to take them, for there is no hope in university professors who are subordinate to millionaires.

But I have declared that Stanford is the most liberal University in all the world. It is the youngest, and is not trammelled by traditions. It is free from prejudice, and its teachers are independent and progressive. Moreover, it stands for the search for truth and justice also, which it is sure to find. It makes for more and better life among men by exposing and denouncing error and injustice wherever they are found. If not yet an advocate of industrial freedom and the Single Tax, it must ere long become so, because all its professors are young and unprejudiced men of pre-eminent ability, honesty, and candor, untrammelled by authority, and unchecked in speech, and, above all, because they are nobly supported by a wise and open-minded chief, who is not only prepared but anxious to follow the teachings of both truth and justice to the very end, even when those teachings overturn his own convictions,and reverse himself. Once let the professors of Stanford remove the bandage which now prevents them from seeing the scales of social justice; once let them see that the balance is uneven, that one scale is weighted down by the privilege of landlordism and the incubus of concentrated wealth, whilst the other is raised by poverty, ignorance and bare subsistence wages almost out of sight of earth and all its benefits, and I believe that Stanford will be the first University to exert its power to restore equality, and make the balance even. Then, and then alone, will justice be equivalent with truth, and truth with justice also.

Note 53.—This kind of misuse of terms hurts the real force of your argument. That the least offensive form of taxation is through land rental I am inclined to think true.   (J.)

This is an excellent conclusion.   (S.)

Note 54.—It is best to omit metaphor in scientific argument, just as in the multiplication table, laws being many, as in medicine. (J.)

No one is able to apply metaphor to the multiplication table, nor to exclude its use in science. So long as the constant facts and definite sequences are there, it really matters very little whether what we call them, but it must of necessity be metaphor. It seems to me that "natural law" as opposed to "human law" is best. It is obviously dangerous to speak of laws in medicine, for only a few have been definitely ascertained, but there can be no doubt whatever that man is a land animal, that is, that his life is maintained by definite conditions supplied by land. (Vide Note 12.)

Note 55.—It is wrong to break agreements or contracts if chiefly the innocent shall suffer, they who trusted to our contracts. (J.)

It is a thousand times worse to let millions of our brethren suffer from injustice and its inevitable consequences—starvation, misery and death —than to inflict mild injury on a comparatively few, who have long enjoyed untold advantages from contracts which neither party had any just right to make. (S.)

Note 56.—We do not know enough to define such a basis to be used in deductive argument as well rest on pure water, freedom, sleep and absolute prohibition. (J.)

This is a matter of opinion, but the real question is, Do the ascertained sequences involved in the maintenance of independent and collective human life define the origin of individual and collective wealth, and determine the rights of the respective owners in its distribution?

Note 57.—It takes a thousand things to make a Utopia. Industrial elements are only part. Utopia, in Mexico, is where no one has to work, and go to a fair every week. In an ideal condition there would be no majority vote or collective action except as men strove to help each other. (J.)

And yet you told your students that unless our souls dwell in Utopia, life is not worth the keeping. But in Nature's Utopia there will always be a struggle between good and evil. It is the contest between the forces which would destroy and those which would uphold which keeps the planets in their orbits, and hangs the constellations in the firmament. Without temptation, virtue would expire (Ingalls). The choice between good and evil must be therefore open to all men in the best Utopia. Nevertheless it is well that our windows should look toward Heaven rather than the gutter, even though we should fail to escape completely from the paternalism of a non-representative, though elected tyranny, or fail to reach the acme of a just republic. In fact, we must be satisfied if true majorities can be made to rule. (S.)

Note 58.—But democracy can handle few things wisely; it promotes public interest and intelligence at the cost of wisdom and persistence. I am converted to proportional representation and an elected oligarchy as a choice of evils. (J.)

Tyrants and plutocrats handle few things better than democracy, and neither wisdom nor persistence can compensate for any sacrifice of public interest and intelligence. No representation is worthy of the name unless it be proportional, and no oligarchy can be effective unless personal responsibility is entirely replaced by corporate responsibility truly representing the power of the people.

To sum up the results of this correspondence, I agree with you that practically we are not far apart. We agree that true representation depends on proportional voting and a pure and effective ballot. That government must be wholly by an elected, untrammelled oligarchy. That the taxation of land values is wiser than the taxation of industrial exertion, and although you do not yet see your way to the complete relief of individual industry from all taxation, I am satisfied that you must eventually come to that conclusion. When individual industry shall once be freed, nothing will be left for taxation except land made valuable by the population.

I confidently anticipate that you will lend the influence of your great name, and that of the institution over which you so effectively preside, in favor of these great reforms, which lie at the foundation of all social progress.　(S.)